Noble Thief

The True Story of Robin Hood

M. Lynn

Edited by Melissa Craven
Proofread by Patrick Hodges
Cover by Covers by Combs

ALSO BY M. LYNN

Legends of the Tri-Gard

Prophecy of Darkness

Legacy of Light

Mastery of Earth

Fantasy and Fairytales

Golden Curse

Golden Chains

Golden Crown

Glass Kingdom

Glass Princess

Noble Thief

Cursed Beauty

The New Beginnings series

Choices

Promises

Dreams

Confessions

Dawn of Rebellion Trilogy

Dawn of Rebellion

Day of Reckoning

Eve of Tomorrow

For Mom and Dad.
Your support is always the most important part of anything I do.

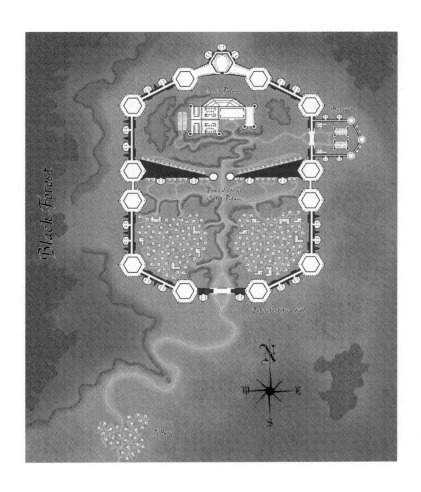

THE CASTLE OF GAULE

Chapter One

Amalie Leroy should have been used to spending her nights in the wild, but something about their mission still tugged at her. Darkness cloaked their movements as they passed through the shadowy trees.

It didn't feel right.

Not what they were about to do—that was the right thing, but she couldn't shake the feeling it was all going to go horribly wrong. Why this night? They'd done this same thing many times before and returned home safely before the sun rose.

To the east lay the village on her estate. Yes, hers. She was Amalie Leroy, daughter of the traitorous duke who led his villagers in a battle against the crown in order to keep magic from their kingdom. Now, she was the only resident of their grand family home.

What was a noble lady doing skulking about in the night? Why was she surrounded by commoners—some of them once-crooks?

Because she had no other choice. She had to make up for the pain her family caused.

And that village to the east? They were starving. All of Gaule was starving while the fat nobles ate at their pleasure.

Pulling her hood up to hide her chestnut hair, Amalie glanced to the man at her side.

He shot her a grin as if this was all great fun.

"John," she hissed. "We've come across no tracks in the last hour. Are you sure this was the route they took?"

He gave her the same look he'd been giving her since they were children running through the village. It was an eyeroll meaning "think before you speak, Amalie."

Rain drizzled through the canopy overhead as Amalie scanned her surroundings. She'd been friends with John since she was six years old. Her father tried to stop the association with the orphan village boy, but at times, they were all each other had.

Until Tyson... she shook her head, needing to erase him from her mind. At least for the night. She could think about him tomorrow, as she always did after nights like this one.

Her feet stuck in the mud with each step and it oozed around her book as she tried to move. "The mud is covering their tracks."

John nodded, pride showing in his eyes. He was a few years older and had always acted like a big brother, teaching her to track and to hunt. When she'd decided to find a way to feed her people, he hadn't hesitated in joining her. In fact, it was his idea to feed them this way.

"They'll have ridden through the night." Tuck, positioned near the front of their group as he always was, bent down to examine something on the ground. He straightened and held up a curved metal horseshoe. "With any luck, it's one of the wagon beasts'."

Amalie pushed through her band of men to Tuck's side, reaching for the muddy shoe he offered. The young friar had joined them when she'd needed someone to help her make sense of the life she'd chosen.

She lifted her eyes to meet his. "We've got them."

Tuck's mouth curved up in a smile, and he nodded. "That we do, my lady." He sometimes insisted on the formal title, knowing it bothered her. After a year of having Tuck by her side, she realized it was just who he was.

"Come on." Amalie led the band through the twisted woods. "They'll have made for the village for a new shoe. We need to catch them on the road." She pulled her bow from where she'd strapped it to her back.

Over three years ago, she'd had her first taste of battle when she rode through the Gaulean palace gates to face her father, to protect those with magic. And again, when she joined Alexandre Durand as he led a small group to Dracon to aid in the fighting there.

She'd had no skill, no knowledge.

But in the years since, she'd trained until her fingers couldn't draw a bow any longer. She'd hardened her body and her mind. She'd become a warrior, fighting for her people, giving up everything dear to her to protect them.

The caravan they searched out carried an entire shipment of food to the Ferenz estate in the west. The Leroy lands were in the center of Gaule, positioned to pick off any shipments that passed through. And she enjoyed enraging Duke Ferenz, the man who'd taken control of the Moreau lands, forcing the duchess from her ancestral home.

At the edge of the trees, they saw them. Four heavily laden wagons rumbled in the distance. The roads of Gaule weren't safe for anyone so waggoneers no longer made camp each night. They slept in the back of moving wagons and ate on the road.

"Do you see any guards?" Amalie asked.

John shook his head. "That's strange, right?"

Royal guards avoided entering the village. They received a cold welcome and suspicion. Amalie smiled to herself, enjoying the thought of her people keeping the guards away

As much as she once loved the royal family, she'd never trust them or their guard again. They'd allowed Gaule to descend into hunger and chaos.

Amalie lifted her bow, tracking the waggoneers with one eye closed. She lowered it, knowing they were too far even for her. "I'm just as likely to kill as wound at this distance."

"Ames." John urged. "We can't lose them." Before she could stop him, he lifted his own bow and released an arrow.

The moment froze in time as they watched the arrow arch through the sky, disappearing in the dark.

A scream echoed from the torch bearing waggoneers. Amalie didn't smile in satisfaction because worry gnawed at her.

Tuck released a string of curses. "You might have killed someone."

He was right. There was no way to control where the arrow hit at this distance. But John wasn't one to play it safe. That trait had both endeared him to her and made her wary. They were all tired of waggoneers and guards and nobles who took advantage of her people, but her band of men operated under a code. They weren't killers. Or, at least they tried not to be.

"Come on." She jumped to her feet and took off, hoping the darkness would hide her approach.

Her men, following her every order, thundered after her.

Waggoneers, already on high alert from the arrow, yelled as they saw the oncoming horde.

Without slowing her steps, Amalie fired three arrows, each finding their target on the legs of men scrambling for their weapons.

John passed her, dropping his shoulder to ram into a man too slow to draw his sword. The pair dropped to the ground. John took the man's sword and rammed the hilt into his head. The guard stopped fighting and John leapt for another.

Amalie always loved watching him fight. He was more of a brawler than a swordsman. He had to be strong, growing up in a village her father controlled.

They made quick work of the rest of the men until a circle of unconscious figures surrounded them.

Amalie turned to Will, a monster of a man. He wasn't a Gaulean, and she loved him more for it. "Drag these men into the woods. We don't want any bandits to come upon them before they're awake to defend themselves." She examined their wounds. "We will send word to the village for a healer."

"Maiya?" Tuck asked, referring to the Draconian who healed with her inherited magic.

Amalie shook her head. "I don't want her near them. It's too dangerous."

The Madran mercenary nodded and bent to haul a man over his shoulder.

"Ames," John called. "You need to come."

She ran to his side and looked into the face of the man lying before them, horror slicing through her.

Simon.

The queen's own guard. An arrow protruded from his stomach. There was too much blood.

"He's not going to make it." John put a hand on her shoulder.

She shook him off. He didn't know who was in front of them. Of course, he didn't. She'd never talked much about her time at the palace. It was too painful.

"He has to make it." She wiped a hand across her face. Was she about to ruin everything? There was no choice. "Tuck," she called. The lithe man appeared at her side. "Take a horse and get this man to the estate... before he dies." She paused. "We can allow Maiya to help this one."

Unlike John who didn't hide his confusion, Tuck gave a shrug of acceptance and went to unhitch a horse from the wagon.

Amalie's men examined the wagonloads of fruit, cabbage, and grain.

As Tuck and John hoisted Simon onto the horse, a thought came to Amalie.

She pulled John away from the others when Tuck left. "What was Simon doing with a band of waggoneers?"

John's brows drew together. "I'm not sure who Simon is."

She sighed. "That man I sent with Tuck is the queen's personal guard."

His eyes widened before shifting toward the woods. "She sent him to guard them."

She nodded. "And where there's one guard, there's—"

Shouting cut off her words as men broke from the trees, darting across the uneven terrain, dodging rocks and roots like ghosts in the night.

"Get to the village," Amalie yelled.

Their people would protect them.

The guards were on horseback but her band was much closer to the village. Amalie ran as fast as her legs allowed. John never left her side.

Adrenaline pumped through her veins until all she could hear was a rushing wind drowning out the hammering of her heart.

They didn't slow until the dirt road turned into a cobblestone street and squat ramshackle buildings rose on either side. The guards neared, their approach deafening as horse hooves hit stone.

John veered into an alleyway and Amalie followed. He leapt for the edge of a roof, and his legs collided with the side of the building as he hung from the terracotta stones. His wine-colored hair blazed in the night when threw his head back and strained his muscles. Using his feet against the wall, he pulled himself onto the roof before extending a hand down to her.

Amalie didn't hesitate taking it. With his help, she pulled herself up. Her bow clattered to the ground and for a moment, she stopped. But there was no time to retrieve it.

The buildings stood only inches from each other, allowing Amalie and John to escape over the flat roofs.

An arrow sailed toward them, but Amalie ducked, managing to stay on her feet. She sprinted across the rooftops, leaping from one to the next. Up ahead, the buildings parted for an alley. She charged ahead and jumped across the wide gap, rolling as she landed. She popped back up.

Another arrow arced through the sky and a yelp of pain sounded beside her. John fell to his knees, the arrow shaft protruding from his thigh.

"John," she screamed, scrambling toward him.

"Don't stop, Ames," he wheezed. "Don't let them see who you are."

"I'm not leaving you." She glanced back over her shoulder to where two guards had climbed onto the roof.

"You have to. I can't run." He gripped her hand. "What you're doing is good. But if anyone finds out about you, it's over. Who would the people have to protect them then?"

Tears streamed down her cheeks. "John."

"Go."

She placed her forehead against his. "I will come for you. Wherever they take you, I'll come."

He nodded before pushing her away.

Amalie couldn't look back again as her feet took her from

one of the most important people in her life. John was her brother, whether they shared blood or not.

But he was right.

There was more at stake.

The guards stopped when they reached John, letting her fade into the night. She slipped over the edge of the roof at the next alleyway, dangling by her fingertips before dropping to the ground.

Glancing down the street, she saw no further pursuit, so she made her way across the village to the estate house she'd always called home.

She slipped through the street side door to the barracks, allowing her to avoid being seen at the gates. Only her most trusted people knew of her nighttime occupation.

A few men lingered about, but these particular barracks housed only those who were part of her merry band of men, seeking justice in a world that had none. Most had yet to return.

She breathed a sigh of relief as her eyes settled on Will. He rushed forward, wrapping her in a tight hug.

"The others?" he asked.

She shifted her eyes away. "I don't know." She wasn't ready to tell her men of John yet. He was her second in command and truly beloved.

What were they going to do without him?

She walked from the barracks unable to find the words of comfort her people needed. They were ambushed. It wasn't the first time they'd fought on their missions, but it was the first time the guard had been waiting for them.

They were no longer an anonymous group of bandits. The queen had taken notice.

She'd almost forgotten about Simon until she walked into the estate house and crossed the stripped down rooms in the front. She refused to live in an ornate home when her people suffered.

Simon laid in the sitting room with Maiya tending his injuries. Tuck hovered nearby.

Simon's gaze found her, scanning the dark green hood still covering her hair and the outfit that was not fit for a noble lady. Loose-fitting pants that made it easy to run, a cotton tunic, and mud covered boots.

His gaze hardened. "The Hood."

She nodded. There was no use denying it. She'd heard her people use the nickname, but it was with a lot more warmth than Simon currently possessed.

Maiya stood. "My healing took a lot of your energy. You will need a few days to recover."

Simon pushed himself from the couch. "No. I will leave now."

Amalie flicked her eyes to Tuck who'd moved to stand by the half-open door.

"I'm afraid we can't let you do that." Amalie crossed her arms over her chest.

Simon's jaw tensed. "Taking prisoners now, Amalie?"

She saw the accusation in his eyes. He wasn't the first person to think it. Her father had been a traitor, maybe it was in the blood.

But there was a difference. Her father did what he did to serve himself. He betrayed a king who'd only wanted to make life better in Gaule. Now their queen had lost control of the kingdom. Amalie only wanted to end the needless suffering.

Simon wouldn't understand that. His blind loyalty was his greatest fault. Queen Catrine could do no wrong.

She crossed her arms over her chest. "I guess I am." To Tuck, she said, "Get him set up in one of the guest rooms. Make sure he has everything he needs." She flicked her eyes to Simon once more. "Remember, his magic emboldens his strength. I want four men guarding him. Then find your own bed. It has been a long night."

She stepped into the hall with Maiya close behind. The caramel-skinned healer said nothing. She'd lived in Amalie's household for over a year now. She too was the daughter of a traitor. Her father betrayed Queen Etta of Bela in the war with Dracon. He even forced her own betrayal.

After that, the girl felt she had no place in the world. Not in Bela or Dracon. Amalie had the same feeling inside her so she'd taken her in, and now Maiya could read her with a single glance. She knew something was horribly wrong.

And yet, she only waited.

Reality crashed in around Amalie as everything struck her at once.

"John..." Her entire body shook. "The queen's men have him."

Maiya put an arm around Amalie's shoulders, letting her healing magic soothe Amalie's pain.

"Do you know the punishment in Gaule for thievery?" Amalie lifted her face to peer at her friend.

Maiya shook her head.

"Hanging." Like her father. Like her sister.

It seemed she was doomed to watch the people in her life meet the noose one by one.

Only this time, she couldn't let it happen.

"What are you going to do?" Maiya asked.

"Find him." Amalie breathed. "I will find him."

Chapter
Two

Two letters. One fate.

Tyson Durand stared down at the papers in his hands as he sat on the edge of the bed in his small one-room home near the palace of Bela, but he didn't need to read the words to know what they said. He'd committed them to memory.

The first came months ago, almost a year to the day after they'd returned from Madra. Camille, the sister he'd once considered power hungry and cruel, no longer wanted the throne of Gaule.

Their mother had named her heir once Alexandre married and became the king of Bela.

No one thought Camille had been an adequate choice at the time, but she'd grown into a woman they would have supported.

And Tyson... he was more Belaen than Gaulean. The magic running through his veins should have been an automatic disqualifier. The people of Gaule would never support him.

Brother, I know this puts a lot onto your shoulders, Camille had written. *You're the only one of us left to carry on the family rule.* Durands had ruled Gaule for centuries. His mother wasn't of Durand blood, but she'd married one who was.

If he was being honest, Tyson didn't have a drop of Durand blood in him either. His true father was Viktor Basile. But he was raised a Durand. His brother and sister were Durands.

You're the only one left.

He crumpled up his sister's letter. It wasn't a surprise. She was marrying the queen of Madra's brother and staying in the kingdom across the sea. At least she'd have Helena there with her. She may be queen now, but Tyson knew her. She'd watch out for Camille. Madra was known for its scheming ways, and Len would make sure Camille didn't fall into old habits.

Tyson thought of the young queen more often since receiving the letter. Helena never expected to be the queen, yet she did what she must to help her people.

Helena was the noblest ruler Tyson had ever met ... aside from his sister, Etta.

He'd waited patiently for the other letter he held, and it only confirmed his fears. It was a summons to the palace of Gaule. His mother had a plan, she always did.

He didn't know when he'd grown to distrust his mother. Maybe it was when she sold Quinn Rhodipus to his brother after Cole Rhodipus stole the throne of Madra.

Maybe it was when she allowed Gaule to fall to pieces.

She'd lost control, and that was unlike her.

He stared at the summons again. What would she do if he refused it?

Send another.

And another.

She wouldn't give up. Eventually, she'd send Simon across the border to drag him to the place he'd once called home.

He couldn't refuse her. No matter what he thought of her decisions, she was his mother and she'd always protected him.

Footsteps sounded in the doorway of his house. He'd helped build it himself and loved every inch of it. It was time he had his own space. He couldn't live with Alex and Etta forever.

A throat cleared, and he looked up into his sister's sympathetic eyes. Etta was once a cold and seemingly uncaring woman, but the past couple of years had made a difference in her. She was... happy.

It stopped grossing him out that his brother and sister were married the minute he saw them in their new home. Alex and Etta shared no parents, but they each shared one with Tyson.

Etta kicked the door closed behind her and threw herself down beside him on the bed, taking the paper from his hands.

"When did this come?" she asked, scanning the document.

He sighed. "Two days ago."

Her only reaction was a raised eyebrow. None of them had reconciled with his mother after she openly supported the usurper king in Madra.

"Maybe it's time." She passed the paper back to him.

He pushed a hand through his dark hair. "I know. Something is happening in Gaule, and I need to know why my mother has let it fall so far."

Etta pursed her lips. "Ty... being a queen isn't easy even in a kingdom like Bela where the people support my every action. I can't imagine what ruling Gaule must be like. That kingdom has always danced on the edge of a knife, ready to fall into disruption and chaos." She squeezed his shoulder. "I don't want you to go alone, though. It isn't safe. Take Edmund."

"Edmund has refused every mission you've assigned him that would take him away from Estevan." Edmund's boyfriend had suffered many traumas at the hands of his own brother in Madra – Cole Rhodipus, a man who wanted Estevan's throne; a throne Estevan ultimately gave to his sister.

"Stev needs separation," she finished for him. "He gave up

his throne in Madra and hasn't been able to fully settle here because Edmund keeps watching his every move as if he'll break. It's been more than a year and Estevan needs to stand on his own two feet. I'm going to give him a position working for me. He knows how to run a kingdom, and I don't want Edmund hovering."

"So, you're making me deal with Edmund?"

She nodded. "Please... just take him." The corner of her mouth curled up. "Before I tie him up with vines and hang him over the cliff just so I can get peace and quiet in my house."

Tyson almost laughed at that, but he didn't find humor in many things lately. Etta had the magical ability to make things grow. It wouldn't be the first time she used her powers on Edmund, but he usually deserved it. He may have his own home with Estevan, but he spent just as much time imposing on Etta's.

Tyson sighed and Etta grinned. They both knew Tyson felt better with Edmund by his side. Over the past few years, he'd been his best friend, the only person who didn't ask him why returning to Gaule whenever his mother asked hurt him so much. He seemed to understand without Tyson having to say her name.

Amalie.

Tyson laid back to stare at the ceiling, his chest constricting. "I guess I'm going to Gaule."

Etta laid beside him and bumped his shoulder. "Hey, you know it'll be okay, right?"

He snorted. "You always say that."

"And I'm always right." She was quiet for a moment. "Maybe when you're there you can—"

"Don't finish that sentence." He knew what she'd been about to say.

"I don't understand any of it, Ty. You and Amalie..."

He cringed at the sound of her name.

Etta continued. "I was sure you two would last forever."

He had thought so too.

He'd fallen in love with Amalie Leroy when she was betrothed to his brother, Alex. She'd become his friend first, exploring the castle at his side. She'd fought beside him in battle and risked her life for his.

He would have done anything to keep her safe.

"Etta—"

She gripped his arm. "Edmund told me about the last time you saw her."

They'd taken Helena and Dell to Amalie's estate because Dell was mortally wounded and needed the magic of a healer in Amalie's residence.

"He said there was a lot of anger between you two. I've seen you change over the last two years, Ty. You've gone from the happy boy I knew to a man with hardness in his eyes and drink in his belly."

He turned onto his side to face his sister. They hadn't grown up together, but he felt like he'd known her his whole life. "I know you're worried about me, but I'm okay."

"Do you promise?"

He nodded.

She closed her eyes for a moment before sitting up. "I won't keep asking you about it, Ty, but I hope you know I'm here for you."

His lips tilted into a rare smile. "Will you tell Edmund you're kicking him out of the kingdom, or shall I?"

Before she could answer, Tyson's door burst open and a panicked Alex rushed in. Etta sat up. "What's wrong?"

Alex's eyes flicked around the room as if searching for something he knew wouldn't be there. "Viktor. He's gone."

"Gone?" Etta jumped to her feet. "What do you mean gone?"

One of the few things Tyson enjoyed lately was watching Etta and Alex obsess over their new son, named for her father.

Alex ran a hand through his hair, making it stand on end. "I left him asleep in his room and walked out to the stables because Vérité was kicking his stall. After I fed the beast, I did more work in the barn. By the time I returned to Viktor's room, he'd disappeared. This is why I keep saying it's time to have guards stationed at our home."

Etta's jaw clenched as worry entered her gaze. "Okay, don't panic. We can't panic."

Alex's eyes widened. "Don't panic? Our son is gone. It's the perfect time to panic. We have too many enemies."

Etta shook her head. "No one from Dracon or Gaule could get through Bela unseen. We'd have heard about it."

"Well, then where is he?" Alex yelled.

Tyson scooted to the edge of his bed. He knew exactly who had Viktor. Who always took him. But Etta and Alex weren't of sound mind.

They didn't notice Tyson pushing past them into the sunlight beyond his door. The seaside village bustled around him. Carts full of fish and grains rumbled down the road, pulled by raggedy looking horses.

Shopkeepers did their best to attract customers, wafting smells out onto the streets. Tyson's stomach growled, but he didn't stop. He reached the end of the road and turned the corner into an alleyway leading to a door he knew too well.

He pushed it open without knocking to find a laughing Viktor lying on the fur-lined rug on the floor. Edmund hovered over him, tickling his sides and muttering nonsense in a voice he'd never want anyone to hear.

Tyson shut the door. "Again, Edmund?"

Edmund glanced up, not surprised by Tyson's presence. He only shrugged before returning his attentions to the baby.

Tyson crossed his arms. "You realize he's Alex's baby, right?" Tyson counted in his head, waiting for the door to open again. Etta and Alex only needed a calm moment to think before realizing where they'd find their son. The door opened, but Tyson didn't turn.

Edmund kept his gaze on the kid. "Alex is a boring old man who doesn't snuggle this baby enough."

Alex cleared his throat.

Edmund still didn't look at them. "Yes, Viktor. I know your papa can hear me. It doesn't make it any less true. Aren't you glad your uncle Edmund is around?"

"Edmund." Etta sighed. "You can't keep taking him."

Edmund lifted Viktor from the floor and cradled him against his chest. "I'm his uncle. If I walk in to your house and find him awake, I can't just walk away. He was looking at me with these eyes that said 'snuggle me'."

Tyson suppressed a laugh. Snuggle me?

Alex held out his arms, but Edmund shook his head. "You're just jealous of my snuggles."

"Stop saying snuggle, Edmund." Tyson covered his mouth with his hand.

Edmund shielded the baby from them and whispered "Don't listen. I love snuggles."

"He's my son." Alex stepped forward. "I want to snuggle him."

Etta couldn't hold in her laugh as she leaned into Tyson and dropped her voice. "Are they fighting over baby snuggles right now?"

Tyson nodded. "Sure you want me to take Edmund? This is entertainment."

"Please. Just get him out of here. This is the third time he's absconded with Viktor this week claiming uncle duties."

Another presence loomed in the doorway. "Edmund." Estevan sighed. "Give the queen and king their son back. We've gone over this. Uncle duties don't give you the right to steal children."

Finally, Edmund relented. "When he grows up and loves me more than the rest of you, it'll be your fault." He set the baby in Alex's arms.

Etta stepped away from Tyson. "Now that we've solved the great uncle crisis, you're heading to Gaule with Tyson."

Edmund gave Tyson a shocked look. He knew more than most what lay in Gaule. There was a lot Tyson never told him though. About his time there. About Amalie. But Etta was right. He needed Edmund with him.

Edmund always had his back. Tyson never knew his true father and his mother was a distant queen now, but he was surrounded by people who loved him.

Amalie Leroy never had such a family.

Before heading into Gaule, Tyson had to clear her from his mind. He wouldn't be going near the Leroy estate. It was time he stopped dwelling on his past because Amalie Leroy had no place in his future.

Chapter Three

Three Years Ago

War ages a person.

Tyson felt every one of his sixteen years and many more. In Gaule, most commoners would be married at his age. They'd spend their days working the fields or manning their shops and then go home to a family. Each day would be the same.

But not for a prince who didn't know which kingdom was his. He was raised as the son of the Gaulean king only to discover his true father was none other than Viktor Basile, descendant of the Belaen kings.

He had magic, but still didn't know where he belonged. Among the magic folk?

An arm wound around his waist and he relaxed his stance to let Amalie into his moment.

"Why are you out here all alone?" Her voice calmed the darkness inside him, washing away the confusion in his mind. He knew where he belonged. With her.

"It's hard to think around the noise." He closed his eyes, listening to the waves crash along the shore.

She leaned in to him, letting the silence sink into their bones.

Only a week ago, Tyson rode beside his sister, Etta, as she faced the sorceress, La Dame. They'd won, but it hadn't come without cost. He'd thought everything was lost. He'd lost faith in Etta. In himself.

And then the wall crumbled to the earth and on the other side was Alex. His brother had come. Behind him was a small Gaulean contingent. Amalie rode at his side. She'd faced the worst thing any of them had ever seen. For him.

He tightened his grip on her. If he hadn't known it before, he'd realized it then.

Amalie Leroy was his future.

They'd never crossed the line between friendship and... more. Growing up, she'd only been Alex's betrothed. Then she became Tyson's companion in many of his misadventures.

"Amalie," he whispered.

She stopped him with words of her own. "We should return to the party."

Away from the beach, in the little town they'd created in Bela, the people celebrated their return home. They mourned those they lost and rejoiced in having a kingdom of their own, safe from foreign rulers.

Amalie turned to leave, but Tyson grabbed her hand to stop her. It was a new life post La Dame. Their world had fallen down around them and yet here they stood. Maybe it was their chance.

"Ames." He tugged her back toward him, and she turned.

Dark eyes peered up at him, lit only by the silver starlight.

Her lips parted as she released a breath.

His lips curved into a smile. "I-I'm not sure I'm truly a prince anymore."

Her brow arched.

He went on. "I have nothing. No house to call my own. Not a gold piece in my pocket." He squeezed her hand tighter. "My only skill, that of the sword, is no use in peace time."

Amalie's laughter was like music punctuated by the drumming of the sea. "Ty, I can honestly say I have no clue where this is going."

"Just listen, okay?"

She nodded.

"I am nothing. Not anymore. But Amalie..." His hand drifted up her arm and over her shoulder until his fingertips skimmed the curve of her neck.

Amalie's smile fell as the words hung between them, both said and unsaid. She dug her fingers into his shirt and pulled him forward.

"You're wrong, Ty." Her words were only a whisper against his lips. "You could never be nothing."

When she kissed him, Tyson believed. In the future. In himself. The war was over and there were so many possibilities. One thing had never changed. He loved Amalie Leroy.

Chapter Four

Present

Home. It was a strange word, implying a warm feeling of comfort. As Tyson glanced up at the towering walls of the palace he'd once called home, wariness sat in his stomach like a stone.

The last time he visited the Gaulean castle, he escorted the princess of Madra on a quest to save her brother.

So much had happened here and not much of it good.

Edmund rode up beside him. "The palace of Gaule is so grand, yet I'd rather ride toward the small home Etta calls the Belaen castle."

Tyson didn't take his eyes from the wall as a foreboding stirred in his chest. "Me too."

Edmund wasn't happy about leaving Stev, but—as Tyson knew it would—his duty overrode personal feelings. Stev had pleaded with him to go, to keep Tyson safe. He said he owed it to Ty after how much he'd risked to put Helena on the Madran throne.

Tyson didn't see it that way. He'd needed something to fight for. It didn't matter it was a foreign princess battling with one of her brothers or that Etta initially said Bela didn't belong in the war. She'd eventually come around and done what he knew she would.

Unlike his mother.

Ignoring Edmund's chatter beside him, Tyson rode through the open gates. The outer castle teemed with activity. It operated much like a village with shops and rows of houses. His horse knew the way because he'd been there many times over the last three years. At the stables, a lad he didn't recognize took the horse from his care, leaving Tyson to walk through the inner gates on foot.

A row of guards lined the inner wall, recognizing him. They made no move to stop him. A few men Edmund knew at the stables had stopped him to welcome his return. Tyson didn't wait. Edmund would catch up.

Familiar walls greeted Tyson with shadows of the past. Tapestries that had hung in the halls since he was a child marked his way.

Outside the castle walls, Gaule was almost unrecognizable with its constant rebellions, dangerous roads, and starving people. But inside, all seemed right with the kingdom. Was this how his mother insulated herself from the problems facing her people? Did she stay among the paintings depicting great victories and prosperity, imagining they resembled the present world?

The serving staff seemed smaller than before, but people still bustled through the halls going about their morning tasks.

He'd visited enough to know his mother's routine never changed. At this hour, she'd be sitting in the throne room, allowing select people to bring forth their troubles. It was a practice she'd adopted only after the battle with La Dame. She wanted to seem as if she truly cared about them.

The sad thing was, Tyson didn't know if she actually did. The crown had changed his mother. She'd transformed from the loving woman she once was into a cold and unfeeling ruler he no longer recognized.

Two guards nodded to Tyson and allowed him entrance into the throne room. His eyes found his mother. She sat on the throne, her back straight, her eyes hard. In front of her stood a gaggle of Gaulean commoners.

The queen nodded, seemingly deep in thought, before addressing a woman nearby. "I understand your situation and will have my people look into it. The bandits will be apprehended."

The woman thanked her, and the queen stood, her eyes sweeping the room. When they landed on Tyson, a spark of life entered them. It was gone just as quickly, and he wondered if he'd imagined it.

"I'm afraid that is all we have time for today." She stepped off the raised platform and two guards escorted her to a private entrance at the side of the room.

"Sir," a guard approached Tyson. "The queen has requested you come with me."

Tyson nodded and followed him without a word. He didn't need an escort. He knew where his mother was having him meet her. The private royal residence seemed so devoid of life with only the queen living there. Once upon a time, Tyson had shared the hall with his brother, sister, and both his parents. Even Etta lived there for a while.

His heart hurt for his mother and sudden regret had his steps speeding up. He'd dreaded returning home, forgetting his mother was all alone.

The guard knocked at the door to the queen's sitting room before pushing it open. Tyson stepped inside, his eyes scanning the familiar surroundings. His mother stood with her back to him fiddling with a tray of mugs.

It was rare to get a moment alone with her. Duchess Moreau and Simon were her constant companions, but he'd seen neither of them.

The door closed behind him with a definitive slam. Tyson clasped his hands behind his back and waited for her to acknowledge him.

When his mother turned, she held a mug in each hand. "Tea?"

Tea? That was the first thing she had to say to him after all that had happened? The problem was, he didn't have the words either. All he could do was step forward and accept the mug.

He studied her over the rim as he took a sip. Dark circles ringed her eyes where they sank into her lined face. She'd gained weight and her beautiful dark hair had streaks of gray.

His mother broke their gaze and walked to the settee facing a glowing fire. A chill setting into his limbs, Tyson followed her.

The weather had turned warm after a long winter, but the stone palace of Gaule always seemed cold no matter the season.

He'd sat on the same chairs many times before talking with his mother of every topic imaginable. They'd been close, and it hurt to feel the distance between them now.

He sat in a high-backed chair and set his cup on the table beside it before crossing his legs.

His mother set aside her tea as well. "It's good to see you, Boy."

He wanted to tell her he hadn't been a boy since the day she told him of his true parentage.

But he didn't. Instead, he forced a smile. "I'm glad to be home, Mother." Lies.

She pursed her lips. "Tyson, let's not pretend this is your home any longer. You only come when you have no other choice."

He could have tried to refute her words, but he was so tired of lies. Instead, he lowered his gaze. "I'm sorry, Mother."

Her expression softened. "I know you are, dear. A lot has happened and we can't change the past. I know what those in Bela and Madra think of me, but I've only ever done what I thought was right."

He sighed. He knew she thought that. But what was right or wrong? Who got to decide what constituted as such?

"Gaule is in trouble, Tyson." She leaned forward, folding her hands on her lap.

"That's an understatement."

Her lips tugged down. "Bandits roam the roads, cutting off supplies to the villages and killing my people. The royal guard now combs the countryside to keep the kingdom safe from those who would throw it further into chaos."

"The guard?" Tyson scoffed. In his father's day, royal guardsmen were no better than the bandits themselves.

His mother raised a brow. "These are my people, loyal and obedient. It is not the days of old. Every time they hang a thief, another comes to light. It is out of control."

Tyson rubbed his chin. "I'm not sure what this has to do with me. Didn't you call me here because of Camille?"

Surprise etched across his mother's face. "Tyson, I know your feelings about Gaule. I would never force the throne upon you." She reached for his hand but thought better of it and pulled back. "Gaule would never accept a Belaen as king."

Tension that had coiled in Tyson's belly since reading the letter from Camille unraveled and he felt as if he could breathe again. "You need an heir, Mother."

His mother's hand rubbed over her stomach. "And I will have one. I do not plan on dying for many years yet."

"No one ever plans..." He froze. "You're..."

She nodded. "Tyson, I'm pregnant."

A wave of relief washed over him. Another child. One they'd raise to rule Gaule. A brother or sister. He closed his eyes for a moment. "That's wonderful news."

When he opened his eyes, he noticed the glassy quality of hers and went to her, sinking into the settee. "What's wrong, Mother?" When she didn't answer, he tried again. "Why have you summoned me?"

When she lifted her eyes to his, a tear tracked down her cheek. "You're the only one I trust to find him."

"Find who?"

"Simon. He's missing."

Chapter Five

She shouldn't be there. The palace was no longer a welcoming place to Amalie Leroy. She'd once been as a daughter to the queen. But that disappeared when they disagreed on her people's fundamental rights and the way to achieve justice. It vanished when the royal guard seized her father's estate, law or not.

Amalie no longer trusted anyone in power. They all had motives beyond the wellbeing of ordinary citizens.

She sat in the hall, eating too-rich foods beside guards and servants. There was another place for nobles and their parties to dine, but Amalie no longer thought of herself as one of them. To their eyes, she was Lady Leroy, always clad in beautiful gowns and adorned with jewels.

But in her mind, the only identity that mattered was the Hood.

A wall at the back of the hall depicted the kingdom's most wanted criminals. The Hood's image had no distinguishing features. The drawing, hanging among images of murderers and traitors, was of a man with a shadowy face.

Amalie stared into the stew before her, a similar dish to the food she served at her estate rather than the fancier meals the nobles would eat. She never wanted to have more than her people did.

Tuck let out a belch beside her. At one time, she'd have flinched, but now she spent most of her life surrounded by vulgar men. He smoothed a hand over his sun-kissed hair and smiled in apology. She shrugged as she shoveled another spoonful into her mouth.

If only her father could see her now.

What would the great Lord Leroy think of his youngest daughter sitting among the common workers? What would her sister, Liza, say about her desire to make Gaule livable for the average man or woman?

Nothing. Because they were dead. Hanged as traitors to the crown. Amalie didn't miss her father or her sister. She'd never known her mother as she'd died in childbirth.

So, it was just her. Once, she'd thought she was all alone.

She'd been wrong.

Commotion near the arched entryway jerked her from her thoughts as a recognizable blonde head ducked through. Amalie shrank in on herself. No one had told her Edmund was present at the castle.

From the looks of it, he'd just arrived.

His voice boomed across the open space as soldiers greeted him. "It sure is cold out there."

Amalie watched the excitement surrounding her old friend, willing him not to spot her. He'd always been popular in the castle but returned home seldom these days.

Home. This wasn't his anymore. He was not a man of Gaule.

As if her thoughts reached him, Edmund met her gaze. He froze for a moment, surprise widening his eyes, before a wide grin spread across his face. "Amalie Leroy," he bellowed.

The surrounding soldiers turned to stare at her, no doubt recognizing the family name of the notorious traitor. She'd hoped to go unnoticed while at the palace, have an audience with the queen, and then leave with John in tow.

So much for that plan. With a sigh, she pushed herself up from the table. Tuck, ever the watch dog, stood at her side.

"You know him?" He nodded toward Edmund.

"Yes."

Edmund reached them and pulled her into a hug before she could stop him. He squeezed so tightly she worried her eyes would pop out of her head.

It wasn't that she didn't like Edmund. In fact, her fondness for him knew no end. But being near him reminded her of what she'd once wanted. What she'd given up.

She pushed at his chest and he released her.

"What are you doing at the palace?" He brushed a strand of hair out of her face. "Ty told me you no longer came here."

Hearing his name sent a chill up her spine. She stepped closer to Tuck, reminding herself that he and John were her present and future. Edmund and Tyson represented the past.

If Edmund knew she spent her nights running through the woods chasing unsuspecting traders, he'd never look at her the same way.

But everyone would find out why she'd come as soon as she spoke to the queen.

Edmund, as if sensing her discomfort, reached for her hand. "I'm not hungry anymore. Let's go."

He led her out of the hall and through the entryway, pushing out into the starlit night. Tuck followed. Out in the courtyard, only a few guards lingered. Edmund dropped her hand and sat on the step, leaning his back against the stone barrier. He said nothing, but his eyes never left her face.

Avoiding his obvious question, Amalie asked one she'd already heard the answer to through rumors spreading across Gaule. "I heard congratulations are in order."

He raised a brow.

"Last I saw you, the princess of Madra was looking for a way back to her kingdom. I've heard she now sits on the throne and suspect you had something to do with that."

He shrugged. "Actually, it was mostly her. She wasn't given that crown. She took it."

"And you saved the boy." Amalie smirked.

Edmund's expression turned sheepish. "Well... Stev."

She grinned. "Are you blushing, Edmund?"

"No." He turned his head so she couldn't see his face any longer, and she laughed.

After a beat of silence, Amalie gestured beside her. "This is Tuck."

Edmund pinned her with a stare again. "Now that we know who everyone is, tell me why you're here."

Amalie sighed and hugged her arms across her chest as she sat on the step above Edmund. "A friend of mine has been arrested."

Edmund jerked his head back in surprise. "I did not expect that answer."

Worry had her tugging the ends of her hair. What was happening to John in those dungeons? Had they tended to his wound? "He was caught stealing from a group of traders."

Sympathy entered his gaze. They both knew what happened to thieves.

"Why are you here?" Her voice shook as her mind stayed with John.

Edmund spoke as if she should have known the answer to her own question. "I came with the prince."

The prince.

Tyson.

He was here.

The blood froze in her veins as her heart refused to pump in its shattered state. She sucked in a breath and her lungs expanded painfully. The last she'd seen him was months ago when Tyson showed up at her door. If it weren't for the wounded man with him, she would have turned him away.

But here, in the palace where they first became friends, it felt as if seeing him would break the remaining parts of her soul. As if it would unravel every long held secret inside her.

Long fingers slid against hers as Edmund gripped her hand. "Hey, you okay?"

She thought she nodded but wasn't sure if she'd managed the movement.

Edmund tapped a finger under her chin and tilted it up so she had no choice but to look at him. "Amalie, what happened between you and Tyson?"

She shook her head. "He never told you?"

Edmund sighed. "About two years ago, Tyson stopped journeying into Gaule. He would no longer visit his mother unless she summoned him. He ceased speaking of you. But it was more than that... Amalie, it was like he stopped living. I was away in Madra for much of that time, but when I returned, he wasn't the same man I'd known."

The words should have comforted Amalie, knowing he'd had as hard a time as she had after everything he'd done, but instead, a tear slid down her cheek.

She pictured the young prince's smiling face as he raced through the castle tunnels when they were children. The way his cheeks grew red when he looked at her. His mindless determination to protect those he loved.

He'd been everything she could dream of. But their match hadn't been fate. Their paths weren't meant to intersect. She'd known that the moment he refused to come when she needed him most.

"Amalie." Edmund scooted to her side, and it was only then she realized Tuck had left to give them privacy.

Amalie had never most of her men about her romance with the prince. They wouldn't understand. They knew she'd had someone who let her down, but the man was a mystery. She surrounded herself with people who had only ill thoughts of the crown and the nobility. Except for Tuck. He'd known because he came into her life when Tyson was still there and everything was perfect. Before she'd known perfection didn't last.

Then there was John, the friend she'd counted on when Tyson wasn't there for her. He never brought up Tyson's name and Amalie had always been grateful for that.

"I don't want to talk about Tyson, Edmund." She tried to shift away from him, but he pulled her closer into his side.

"I've known you too long not to meddle. You're both here, and you obviously still care about him. So, why don't you talk?"

She shrugged off his arm and stood, smoothing down the dress she had to wear to play the part of a lady. "You're wrong, Edmund. Tyson Durand means nothing to me. He never did." The lie was still on her tongue when she turned on her heel and came face to face with the boy she wished she'd never known.

Chapter Six

Three years ago

"I think I could stay like this forever." Tyson sighed in contentment as he smoothed a calloused hand down Amalie's bare back.

She rested her cheek against his chest and traced the ridges of his stomach with light brushes of her fingertips. "I do too. You know why?" She propped herself up on her hands, letting her hair hang about her creamy shoulders as early morning light streaked through the window, illuminating her skin.

He'd never seen anything so beautiful. "Tell me."

"Because I have you right where I want you." She leaned down to press her lips to his. "Under my power."

He smiled against her lips. "Completely under your power. Enthralled. Entranced. Yours."

"Mine." She kissed him again, pressing her chest against his.

A knock at the door stopped their morning before it began. Amalie buried her face in his neck and laughed.

"Breakfast is ready," a gruff voice called in.

"Thank you, sir," Tyson answered. "We'll be there in a few moments."

They listened for his footsteps to fade away. They'd stopped in a border village on their way to the Leroy lands, bringing Amalie home for the first time since her father was hanged.

Much of the village was damaged and many of the people left in the weeks leading to the battle with La Dame, but they'd managed to find an inn.

Amalie rolled off Tyson, and they each pulled their clothes on before stopping at the door for one final kiss.

In the dining room, an older woman greeted them with a smile. "It's always nice having young people in residence who are just beginning their lives together... Even if the walls are thin." She winked.

Tyson laughed, and Amalie slapped his arm as the woman hurried away.

He leaned in. "She thinks we're married."

"And we need to keep it that way."

Tyson wound an arm around her waist. "What if we did it? What if you returned to your father's lands as not only the rightful duchess, but one married to a prince?"

Present

Amalie had never wanted to be a princess. Tyson hadn't considered that at the time but even now, he still didn't know what she wanted.

As he stared at the woman before him, her words bouncing in his mind, he couldn't find a trace of the girl he once knew. The softness of Amalie Leroy was gone, replaced by a woman with hard edges.

Tyson Durand means nothing to me. He never did.

He'd had two years to wonder if what they'd had was real, but being hit with the truth so suddenly sucked the air from his lungs.

Amalie's mouth moved, and he thought she tried to say his name, but he shook his head. The day had gone from bad to worse, and he didn't know how much more he could take.

Simon was missing, and his mother pleaded with Tyson to find him, the guard who also happened to be the father of Tyson's newest sibling.

No one would have claimed his family was ever normal or even sane, but some days, he wished for a different kind of life. One where he could have stayed in the border village where all his dreams had come true. Where he'd fallen in love.

Tyson shook his head and turned to Edmund. "I'm going to find food in the noble's hall. I can't stomach that gruel the guards eat. Not tonight."

A scowl flashed across Amalie's face. "Right. The prince needs his fine foods."

He didn't acknowledge her words. In the years since the rebellions and war with Dracon, Amalie's hatred of the wealthy increased.

Tyson wondered if she realized that she too had noble blood in her. One didn't get to choose the circumstances of their birth.

He turned without another word. Edmund followed soon after.

"I don't want to hear a word about it, Edmund." His friend tried to push him about Amalie, but she no longer mattered. He had bigger worries.

They seated themselves at a short table along the wall and leaned back as a servant filled their wine goblets.

Edmund took a long drink and eyed Tyson. "Out with it. Did Catrine make you agree to take the ever-changing position of Gaulean heir?" He smiled, burgundy wine coating his teeth. "Gaule will fall apart when they learn the new heir is half Belaen... well, more than it's already falling apart."

Tyson studied the plate a servant set in front of him. Roasted fowl and potatoes. If there was one thing he missed about Gaule, it was the food. In Bela, it seemed every meal centered on either venison or fish.

But he suddenly had no appetite.

"My mother is pregnant." He rubbed a hand over his face.

Edmund's grin widened as a laugh slipped past his lips. "Well, that's a surprise."

Tyson ran a hand through his hair. His mother was in her forties. No one expected her to produce another heir. He should've been relieved, but everything else she'd said rolled through his mind. He tried understanding everything his mother told him. She wanted him to find Simon. Many of her guards were on the same mission, but she needed her son to do everything in his power to search out the man she loved.

His mother wanted him to seek out the bandit responsible for terrorizing the supply chains of Gaule. The Hood. Tyson had heard the name last time he was in Gaule. A master archer with nerves of steel, the Hood attacked wagons containing food and other goods, bringing them to the villages. He never killed anyone, but his men were still dangerous.

Releasing a breath, Tyson looked to Edmund. Would his life ever be his own? It seemed there was always some mission that needed his attention.

"It seems I'm going to be staying in Gaule a while," he said.

"As heir?" Edmund's gaze bore into him. He didn't know what it was like to have the responsibility of a kingdom thrown at you, but he loved a man who did. If things had gone differently, Estevan would rule Madra, not Helena.

Tyson shook his head and explained everything he'd learned. About Simon's task. About the Hood.

When he was finished, Edmund set his fork down. "I'll be with you, of course."

Tyson knew he'd say the words. Edmund would always do what was asked of him, always the honorable thing.

He nodded, grateful he wouldn't have to face this alone, because the place where he needed to start was the last place he wanted to go.

The Leroy lands.

The Hood's last known whereabouts.

He'd need Amalie's help, a safe place to stay. He pressed the heel of his hand against his eyes, trying to ward off the coming headache. Most of Gaule held dangers for someone like him, someone with magic.

He had to remind himself it was for Simon, the guard who loved his mother, and his mother deserved even the smallest bit of happiness in this life.

"When do we leave?" Edmund asked.

"As soon as Amalie does."

Edmund looked like he wanted to say something more but stayed quiet as he dug back into his food.

Maybe this would be easier if Tyson could hate her. If he could see her as the self-righteous lady most of the other nobles saw.

But the only image in the spaces of his mind was of a shy girl with the prettiest blue eyes and the warmest heart.

Where had she gone?

Chapter Seven

Amalie's steps echoed off the stone ceiling as she paced in front of the door to the throne room. She'd had to wait two days for an audience with the queen. There was a time when she wouldn't have had to wait at all.

But as lady Leroy, she'd spent the past two years criticizing the crown and distancing herself from the woman who'd once treated her kindly.

If Catrine knew how she spent her nights, or who she had locked up back at her estate, any remaining amount of goodwill would vanish.

How had they gotten here?

It was for John, she reminded herself. All for John.

Her first instinct was to offer a trade. Simon for John. But Simon knew the missions she carried out while the rest of the kingdom slept. He knew the name they'd given her.

Admitting she had Simon would reveal it for all. Even Catrine couldn't stop the noose from tightening around Amalie's neck then.

She would figure out what to do about Simon later. John's problem was more pressing. How did she free him without revealing herself?

The door opened, and a guard stepped through, nodding at her to approach. Inside the throne room, nothing had changed. The same velvet carpeting made a path between pillars to the gold carved throne, worn with age and neglect.

Images flashed through her mind. She saw her father kneeling in front of the fuming Alex. Guards dragging the lords and ladies away. That had been the turning point for Gaule. From then on, many of the nobles lost all faith in the crown.

They increased the size of their own forces, raising rents in the villages to pay for it. They abandoned some of the kingdom's laws in favor of their own. Alex had done the right thing, but Gaule was not a kingdom built on justice, and the quest for equality fractured it into many pieces.

Catrine did more good than Alexandre could have. Amalie admitted that. But she never left the palace. She didn't see the state of her people's lives. Instead, like many of the nobles, the queen stayed in the safety of her home where she was afforded every luxury, while the villages were left with precious little.

Amalie's feet froze when she looked into the queen's face.

Catrine stood and rushed down the steps, pulling Amalie into a warm hug. "Dear girl, it is good to see you."

Amalie nodded, willing back the tears that sprung to her eyes. Wrapped in a motherly embrace, she longed for the time when she'd been part of this family. Before, just like the kingdom they ruled, that had shattered as well. If she hadn't made the hardest decisions of her life two years before, she would be a part of it still.

Reluctantly, Amalie pulled back.

Catrine cupped her cheek. "I wanted to see you as soon as word of your arrival reached me, but I was ill yesterday."

Amalie tried to hold on to the ire she felt toward the woman, but it unraveled too quickly until all she felt was exhaustion. She no longer had the energy for pleasantries.

"Your Majesty," she began.

"Since when do we rely on formalities, Amalie?"

"Since you're keeping a man from my village in the dungeons."

Catrine pursed her lips and stepped back, smoothing her hands over her emerald silk gown. "It seems we must talk business then." She turned and walked back to her throne. As she sat, she waved a hand, gesturing Amalie to come forward as if she were any other petitioner.

Nerves twisted in Amalie's gut, and she wished more than anything she could have her hood and bow. They infused a confidence in her she never felt as a lady of court.

But she'd trained for this her entire life so she pasted on a complacent smile and stepped forward. "Your Majesty, a man by the name of John Little was arrested weeks ago in a village on the Leroy lands. His family is adamant it was a case of mistaken identity."

Lies. John had no family other than her.

Catrine's dark gaze studied Amalie's face. Only torches lit the windowless room, casting an orange glow across their skin.

"John Little." The queen nodded. "Yes, he is here."

Relief bloomed through Amalie's chest. Tuck had searched all the nearby village prisons, even checking the rolls of the hanged, before learning John was brought directly to the palace.

The queen's next words pushed all relief away. "But I cannot release him."

Amalie opened her mouth before shutting it and trying again. "His family—"

"Is lying." She said it so calmly Amalie's anger bubbled to the surface.

"These are good people, Catrine." Her jaw clenched. "Maybe you aren't used to honest, hardworking folk, but they don't deserve to have the crown destroy their lives. Maybe you forget what empathy feels like, but I can't let that happen."

Catrine folded her hands in her lap. "Are you done?"

There were so many other things Amalie wanted to say to the queen, but none of them would help John, so she only nodded.

"Good. Listen to me, Amalie Leroy. I don't know what happened to the obedient, sweet girl I knew—"

"She grew up."

Catrine cut through her with a harsh stare. "The boy you plead for was found with the Hood. I have testimonies from no less than three of my trusted guards. Do you want to know about the bandit your friend was aiding?"

Amalie stood stone still, barely able to breathe.

"The Hood travels the roads at night, looking for unsuspecting travelers. He sets his men upon them to steal what these good people have worked for. People have been injured. We've heard of a few deaths even. But that isn't the worst part. This hooded bowman galvanizes the kingdom, sowing unrest. Do you know how many copy cats we've apprehended?"

Amalie shook her head.

"Eleven. With each arrest, the people grow more uneasy. They turn against the crown when all we want to do is protect them. With La Dame dead and Madra once again stable, our greatest threat now comes from within. This is the time for our kingdom to come together, and the Hood is only tearing it further apart." Her chest heaved with anger.

Amalie's throat constricted as the words struck her with the full force of an accusation. It wasn't her fault others had attacked travelers in her name. She pictured the arrow John had shot into Simon. Yes, people got hurt. A few died. But how many more had lived?

How many families had she fed? The villages across the Leroy and surrounding lands welcomed her men upon sight, knowing they kept their children from dying of empty bellies.

She steeled her gaze. No. The unrest wasn't her fault because the people had many reasons to be discontented.

The queen calmed her breathing, and the anger left her gaze. "I'm sorry about your friend, Amalie. I truly am. I wish I could take the trouble from your mind. But I need to put Gaule first. John Little will hang at first light." She stood. "I'm afraid I must return to my bed. I am suddenly overcome with weariness."

She left Amalie standing in the throne room with only a silent guard for company. Amalie closed her eyes, a tear escaping. She'd failed him. John had always been there for her and because of that, he'd hang.

Tuck waited for her in the room they shared. As soon as he saw her face, he wrapped his arms around her. Once, she'd enjoyed more lavish rooms at this palace with connecting rooms for servants. But that was a long time ago.

"We've lost him, Tuck." The men who pledged their loyalty to her had become her family, and she knew this would break them. It would break her.

The big man sighed. "Not yet."

"What are we supposed to do?"

A slow smile spread across his face. "What we always do. Fight for the ones who can't fight for themselves."

THE DUNGEONS HADN'T CHANGED. Musty air

assaulted Tyson as soon as he descended the narrow stone staircase.

"Have you ever wondered if we spend too much time in these dungeons?" Edmund asked, the humor in his voice masking the hatred Tyson knew he felt for the place.

He wasn't wrong. They had a habit of meeting people in these cells. Edmund had even been locked in one for a while. The last time they'd come had been with Helena, the new queen of Madra, when her brother, Quinn, was held prisoner here, waiting to be sent home to his usurper twin.

Tyson's mother told him they had a man in custody, a man connected to the Hood. He was scheduled to hang in the morning, so Tyson hoped he could convince him to do some good before he died. Maybe he'd want to make up for a life of thievery.

The guards nodded to them, recognizing Tyson, and pointed to a cell near the end of the hall. Despite the prison's full capacity, an eerie hush fell over the place.

They passed the turn that would have taken them to the cell both Etta and Edmund had occupied at different times. It still amazed Tyson to think of everything they'd all been through.

In the final cell, a man sat in the center with his legs crossed and his eyes closed as if in meditation. The first thing that struck Tyson was his youth. He couldn't have been much older than him.

An unkempt beard covered the lower half of his face. How long had he been here?

A tear up the side of his trousers revealed a bandage wrapped tightly around his leg with blood seeping through it.

Edmund gripped the bars in front of them. As if sensing the movement, the man's eyes snapped open.

"John Little?" Tyson asked.

No movement. No sound. The man only stared.

"Answer me."

The corner of the man's mouth tilted up. "I don't know who you think you are, but I only answer to one person."

"The Hood?"

John's eyes snapped to Tyson's. That was answer enough.

Tyson held his gaze. "Have they told you you're due to hang in the morning?"

"And you think that means I'll talk to you, Prince?"

Tyson rubbed his jaw. "So, you do recognize me."

"Of course I do. I saw you once before when you lived at the Leroy estate. You Durands think Gaule owes you everything; that the common people deserve less. I don't care what happens to me. I will never help you."

His sentiment sounded eerily similar to the words Amalie had once flung at him.

Tyson clenched his jaw. "The Hood is nothing more than a criminal. You're loyal to a man who will show you no loyalty in turn. He steals, and murders, and abducts people."

John rose up on his knees. "You know nothing of which you speak." He tilted his head. "Have you ever been loyal to someone, Prince? Truly loyal? Someone who infuses the belief that they'll make a better world. That they are the kind of person who will fight until they can't any longer?"

Tyson had been loyal to many people in his life. His mother. Alex. His friends. But there was only one person he'd ever heard spoken of with such reverence. His sister, Etta. The fire in John's eyes was the same he'd seen in Etta's people. He knew then, he'd never get the information he sought. Not from a man whose loyalty had become more. It was love.

Just as Etta's people loved her and believed in her, so too did the Hood's followers. How did a criminal garner such passion?

Tyson turned to Edmund. "We won't get anything out of

him." He marched back through the dungeons, barreling out into the open-air corridor.

Edmund came up behind him. "We barely questioned him."

Tyson shook his head. "He won't be any help." That man back there would be dead in the morning. He'd give his life for this Hooded figure.

Why?

Tyson needed to find out.

Chapter Eight

Amalie would never forget the day her father and sister died. They deserved the traitor's hanging they got, but they were still the only family she had. She was a coward then, refusing to watch them leave this world. She'd hidden in the palace tunnels with Tyson, letting him occupy her troubled mind.

But today was different. Today, she had to be there, to keep her mind on the happenings in front of her even if it tore her heart out to watch.

Officials in the villages hanged many Gaulean citizens across the kingdom over the last few seasons. The royal guard roamed the land, upholding laws and acting as sheriffs over the people.

Amalie stood near the back of the gathering crowd. Their whispers told her word had circulated that one of the Merry Men who followed the Hood was set to die.

And if she knew one thing, it was that people loved a tragedy.

She backed away from the platform, through the throng, her

eyes scanning the market square. She'd once wondered why the hangings no longer took place on the hill near the castle as her father's had.

Then she learned the truth. The crown cared more for perception than justice. They wanted the punishments to be seen as given out by the people, by the officials in the villages, rather than the queen herself or her guards.

Tuck nodded from the doorway of a nearby shop, and Amalie quickened her step. Inside, a pungent scent hung in the air. Jars of herbs lined every surface, mixing their odors.

"This is David Caster." Tuck gestured to the older man rearranging jars near the window.

Amalie studied him. Before joining her, Tuck was a traveling friar. He had those he trusted in every town, every village. But she was cautious.

She bent to peer at a ceramic bowl filled with dried purple leaves. "You an herbalist, David?"

"Yes, my lady." He stood straight but lowered his eyes in respect.

Tuck reached behind a table, revealing a bow and quiver of arrows. It put Amalie at ease, providing her with some semblance of control. With a bow in her hand, she decided what happened next. She reached for it, running her hands along the smooth wood. The lady Amalie couldn't travel with a bow and risk being seen with anything connecting her to the Hood. As far as anyone knew, she was just a helpless noble who relied on people like Tuck and John to protect her.

But they didn't have John this time. She lifted her eyes to Tuck. "Just us then?" None of the others had traveled with them. Most of her band were wanted for some infraction or another and wouldn't be welcome so near the palace. She'd have felt better if they were there.

She flicked her eyes to David, not knowing how much she could trust him.

Tuck eyed him cautiously as well.

Before Tuck could say another word, the door crashed open and a girl burst into the room, red hair flying about her heart-shaped face.

"Uncle," she addressed David, ignoring Amalie and Tuck. "It's true. I saw him. They have one of the Merry Men." Excitement rang in her voice.

Amalie shared an alarmed look with Tuck. It was time.

The excitement wasn't only in the girl. Out on the streets, the mood was palpable. No one had ever been that close to the Hood and John was seen as an extension of the elusive criminal.

Only, these people didn't see the Hood as a criminal. Hushed whispers and awestruck words told a different story. Among the great houses and palaces of Gaule, the Hood was a nuisance, interrupting their otherwise comfortable lives. But in the villages, in the streets, he was one of them. Fighting for them.

What would they think if they knew it was a woman they spoke of? A noble one at that.

Amalie hid the bow and quiver beneath her cloak and moved closer to the platform. She'd exchanged her flared dresses for tight fitting brown trousers and a forest green tunic, loose enough to hide the curves of her body.

A wagon rumbled up with the prisoners chained in the back. Her eyes went to John. His handsome face looked drawn with dark circles under his eyes and an uncharacteristic beard coated his cheeks. Gone was the warmth she knew him for. The easy smiles and kind eyes.

The world had beaten him down. Weeks in a prison cell awaiting one's own execution was the worst kind of torture.

Tuck gripped her elbow and pulled her to the side of the crowd.

"Are you going to be able to do this?" he asked.

She nodded. She had to. They had a plan. Tuck gave her one last long look before leaving to perform his duties. The town's friar had taken to his bed in sickness thanks to an herb from David's shop. So, it fell to Tuck to provide the last rituals for the condemned.

Amalie entered an empty storefront and thundered up the stairs. The window they'd chosen overlooked the day's activities. A few men David trusted agreed to watch the building and be on the alert for anyone following her.

Movement at the back of the crowd caught her attention, and Amalie froze momentarily. Tyson stood with his arms crossed, surveying the scene before him. Amalie couldn't tell what was going through his mind as she peered down from the window. There was a time when she could read him so easily. She'd known everything about him.

Now, a stranger walked in his shoes.

She shook her head and shifted so the giant wooden shutters hid her. The room was obviously lived in with a rumpled bed in the corner and still warm coals in the fireplace. But David had assured Tuck it would be unoccupied.

Amalie would never get used to the high stakes of the game they played. She couldn't count the number of missions she'd led her people on, but the nerves never went away. Plucking her finger against the string of her bow, she waited. Their plan was risky, but it was all they had.

A guard led the prisoners onto the platform and Tuck stepped forward, black robe billowing around his legs.

Edmund stood to the side of the platform as he turned, his eyes seeming to find her hiding place. No, he couldn't see her. Could he? He stared for a moment longer before turning back to the ceremony happening before them. They allowed prisoners a few final words before the friar performed the ceremony of the dead, giving them peace before their last breath.

Amalie didn't hear what any of the other prisoners said as she focused on John. He spoke last.

When he cleared his throat, the entire crowd grew quiet, listening for any word about the Hood.

John stared at them unapologetically. He'd never been ashamed of his station in life. It was one of the things Amalie loved about him.

"I am not innocent," he began. "At least of the things they accuse me of. I have spent the last two years beside the most honorable person I know. The one you call the Hood."

Amalie sucked in a breath as murmuring broke out among the crowd.

"They call us thieves," John continued. "Bandits. Criminals. But it is them who steal from us. They take food from the mouths of our children. The nobles care nothing for us. I am one of you. I grew up with no home, nothing to call my own except my honor. And that is not something they can take from me in death."

A cheer rose up. They rooted for him.

When the hangman put a hand on John's shoulder and jerked him back, the people screamed in protest.

Amalie's heart thudded against her ribs, but John showed no fear. In that moment, the man they called John Little was the giant among them.

Tuck's voice rose above the rest as he addressed each man and allowed them to drink from the chalice he held. Their final rites.

He stepped in front of John. To her friends' credit, neither of them showed any sign of recognition. Their lives rested on their ability to remain anonymous.

"John Little," he began.

Amalie couldn't see his movements but she knew the moment Tuck must have shifted his hand to slip the herb into the chalice. John, with his hawk-like eyes, must have seen it too because he straightened.

But he trusted Tuck.

He took a sip before handing the cup back. Tuck stepped away, giving Amalie the clear view she needed.

Hopefully John would forgive her for what she had to do next.

She pulled an arrow free and rested it against the string of her bow as she flexed her fingers and took a deep breath to still her shaking hands. Edmund, still next to the platform moved, distracting her as she loosed the arrow. His head jerked up to stare at her as her arrow continued its arc. Amalie knew immediately it would miss her intended target.

The crowd screamed, pushing each other out of the way as they scrambled for safety from the supposed attack.

Amalie quickly knocked a second arrow, cursing herself, and set it free. John jerked back, the shaft of wood stuck in his arm. Tuck caught him as he pitched forward, unable to hold himself up any longer.

"It's the Hood!" someone cried. "They've come to keep him silent."

Amalie didn't have time to consider what it meant if the people believed she'd kill her own men. She dropped the bow and sprinted from the room to run down the stairs and out into the crowd.

Missing on the first try lost her precious time. She'd lost her focus and John deserved more than that. What if she'd hit something important? She'd been aiming for a non-life threatening injury, but it all happened so quickly. The herb Tuck had given John would make him appear as if he'd stopped breathing. Her job had been to give them a cause for his supposed death.

She'd meant to shoot her best friend.

And now she only hoped he wasn't truly dead.

She slammed into a solid wall of muscle and hands gripped her shoulders. Glaring up into the eyes of the man who could ruin everything, she ripped herself free. "Let me go."

As she tried darting around him, Edmund yanked her arm back. She reached for the knife tucked into her belt, knowing full well she couldn't use it on her friend.

"Stop," he commanded, pulling her after him into a narrow alleyway and away from the crowd.

"What are you doing?"

"Helping you," he grunted.

Something about his words rang true, and it was only then she realized he didn't mean to turn her in to the queen. She stopped struggling and let him guide her around the corner. Noise from the crowd faded behind them and she looked back over her shoulder. Was John okay? Worry gnawed at her, but she didn't turn back yet.

Edmund reached out and ripped the hood from Amalie's head. "Take that off."

How could she have forgotten she was wearing it? At least anyone at the hanging would have seen the hood, but not the woman behind it.

Edmund shoved the hood at her chest and she stuffed it quickly in the bag hanging over her shoulder. He stopped walking and turned to her.

"Did you even consider how you'd get out of there?" His scowl irritated her. This man didn't know her anymore.

"Of course I did."

He crossed his arms over his chest. "Then I'm sure you knew of the guards who spotted you as soon as you exited the building? Or the villagers who were almost close enough to get a peek underneath that hood of yours?"

Amalie blew a strand of hair out of her face. "Of course." She was lying. In her haste to get to John, she'd grown careless. She'd never been so ill prepared in her life. It was why she was normally so good at what she did. She left her emotions behind.

A thought struck her. "You can't tell Tyson."

He raised a brow.

But she didn't stop. A man she'd barely seen in years now held her life in his hands. If he went to the guards or told the queen her identity, everything would come crashing down.

And if Tyson knew... she shook her head. The self-righteous prince would tell her to stop. He'd never imagine the girl he'd once claimed was too good for her family would skulk around forests, stealing to support her people.

Anger burned through her as Edmund studied her. He hunched his shoulders to peer into her eyes, his tall frame towering over hers.

"Why did you help me?" Her voice had lost some of its confidence.

He blew out a breath. "You really have to ask that, Amalie? I've known you for many years." He closed his eyes for a moment. "What you're doing is dangerous. I've heard the stories of the Hood all the way in Bela."

She narrowed her eyes. "Someone had to feed my people."

He put a hand on her shoulders and peered into her eyes. "I get why you're doing it, but..." He pushed out a frustrated breath. "Fine. I won't tell Tyson, but you need to prepare."

"For what?"

"We've received a mission from the queen. She has asked Tyson to search for the Hood. Apparently, Simon is missing."

She averted her eyes, but Edmund didn't move his hands. "Where is Simon, Amalie?"

She sighed. "Alive. That's all I can tell you. I have to go. My friends are counting on me."

He released her. "Once upon a time, we were your friends too."

At those words, Edmund walked away, back toward the crowd they'd left behind.

But Amalie stood frozen for a moment longer. Tyson was tasked with capturing the Hood—capturing her.

She reached into her bag, curling her fingers in the rough woolen hood, letting it calm her frantic heart. She couldn't control many things, but she would decide what Tyson saw, what he learned.

John's face flashed across her mind. Tyson Durand would have to wait. Another man needed her.

She ditched the bag containing the hood in a corner of the alley, knowing it would be a death sentence to be caught with it. Armed with only a simple dagger in a sheathe at her waist, she left the relative quiet of the alleyway and skirted the edge of the still panicking crowd.

On the platform, two men hung by their necks. They'd decided to go ahead with the executions after all. Neither man was John, and she sighed in relief.

Avoiding the platform altogether, Amalie kept her pace even to avoid the appearance of running from the scene. Hopefully Tuck would be at the rendezvous point with John. Tuck had asked David to procure a cart and horses for them.

It was a fair bit of walking to the edge of the village where a vast plain stretched between them and the dark edges of the Black Forest.

She'd feared the ominous place before she learned there were real monsters that existed outside the stories of a haunted wood. La Dame had been pure evil, but so had Amalie's own father and sister.

Behind one of the houses at the end of town, a small stables housing only a few horses stood, rotting boards leaning in. Moss stretched up the side of the building. Beyond it, black cows lingered in the green pasture.

"Hello, dear." A voice said behind her.

Amalie jumped at the sound before turning to face the plump older woman. Her dusty hair was pulled back into a tight bun. She carried a pail of milk with one hand as she wiped the other on her dirty apron.

"You must be the lady Amalie." The woman's face stretched into the kind of smile Amalie rarely saw anymore. Warm. Sweet.

Spending her life surrounded by men who belonged in a cell as much as in the open had taken most kind interactions from her world. She loved her boys, and they loved her, but no one had spoken to her with such warmth since she'd forsaken Queen Catrine.

Remembering her manners, Amalie returned the smile. "I hope this is the right place."

The woman nodded. "My David said you'd be buying our cart and a couple horses for your travels."

Of course. She wanted paid. Amalie reached into the pouch at her waist, procuring a few gold coins. It was more than a cart and horses were worth, but from the state of the falling down barn and small house, she knew it would be a help. Her father left the estate with fat coffers. If she couldn't help the people who needed it, what good was the money for? She held out the coins.

The woman took a step back. "Oh no. I can't take your money, dear."

"It isn't charity. It's for the cart."

The woman smiled again and reached out. Amalie thought

she'd take the coins, but she folded Amalie's fingers closed and held onto her wrist.

"There are many others who need your help. We get by." She pierced Amalie with a knowing stare.

Panic built in Amalie's chest. She knew. How many people knew of the Hood's identity? It would only take one for it all to come to light.

The woman released her as the rumble of cart wheels reached them. Two horses pulled a wagon that had seen better days. The sides were cracked and splitting. The wheels creaked with each turn.

But that wasn't what caught Amalie's attention. Forgetting about the older woman, she ran toward the cart. It pulled to a stop in front of her. David and the young girl from before sat atop it, steering the horses.

Tuck jumped from the back where Amalie could now see John's form.

"How bad is it?" Amalie asked, rushing to the side. She reached in to feel John's pulse.

Tuck pulled her back. "We won't know until he wakes. The herb makes him appear dead, but he's been wounded badly. I removed the arrow and wrapped the wound quickly, but it will need taken care of with more precision.

"What did we do, Tuck?" She turned her face up to his. "Did we kill him?"

He gripped his shoulders. "He'd have died if we didn't try. At least this gave him a chance. It's only an arm wound. He should live. I worry more about infection setting in from the old wound in his leg."

She shuddered, and he pulled her into his side.

It took her a moment to remember everything that had happened. "I shot him."

Tuck cleared his throat. "You had to."

The girl stepped forward. "I would have never imagined it was a woman. This is... wow."

"You can't tell anyone." Amalie didn't take her eyes from John's serene face. "I need your vow of silence. What happened here today is not to be spoken of."

The girl nodded.

"You have our promise," David said.

Amalie nodded. "We must be on our way. Thank you for your help." She didn't say the words out loud, but they needed to return home before Tyson arrived. She knew the prince almost as well as she knew herself. His mission might be the find the Hood, but he wouldn't be able to resist a visit to her, no matter the chilly reception he received.

Princes were stubborn beasts.

Tuck climbed onto the driver's seat and Amalie pulled herself into the wagon bed beside John.

Before long, the village lay in their past and open road stretched out before them.

Amalie checked the bandage. Tuck wrapped it in a hurt as he rode in the back of the cart, but it wasn't any worse than she would do. Sweat soaked John's hair and Amalie caught a slight movement out of the corner of her eye. His chest rose before going still again.

She placed her finger on his neck, taking comfort in the thumping of his pulse. She hadn't had Tyson on her side in a long time. Her family was dead. Catrine was more queen than friend now. But John... he was always there, picking up the pieces of her life each time they scattered on the winds of change.

***

Three years ago

Home.

Amalie hadn't been back to her father's lands in a long time. No, not her father's. They belonged to her now. From the Eastern river to the grain fields along the edges of the Hinton lands. The village in the south and smaller settlement to the west.

All of it had been in her family for generations.

And they'd failed the people who relied on them.

Amalie rode beside Tyson as they descended the hill leading into the village that had seen better days. Empty storefronts greeted them with shattered windows. People and animals alike sat on street corners, hoping someone more fortunate than them also had a heart.

Amalie was too stunned to approach any of them. She only wanted to get behind the high walls of her estate house. There, she'd find warm fires and a hot meal.

They'd been traveling for days, and it had been so carefree. She'd never been as happy as the last weeks. Tyson made her feel as if she could do anything.

The gates to the estate were closed when they arrived. A man in her family's emerald green colors stepped through a small door. She didn't recognize him, but she'd never made a habit of getting to know her father's men.

"I'm afraid the estate is closed to commoners." The guard widened his stance and rested his hand on the hilt of his sword.

Amalie raised a brow and scanned her eyes over her and Ty's clothing. They looked like commoners in their simple wool pants and tunics. They'd left Bela after the battle with La Dame. It had been a brutal fight in which they almost lost everything. Before reclaiming the duties they couldn't avoid forever, they wanted to just live, to be happy together. The friar and inn keepers they'd stayed with on the border had given them these clothes when he realized they traveled with nothing.

Amalie sat straighter in her saddle. "This estate is never closed to me." She slid down and Tyson followed her. "I own it."

Tyson only chuckled as she pushed past the guard and led her horse through the door at the base of the large gates.

"I need to start saying that," Tyson joked. "Nothing in Gaule or Bela is closed to me because I own them both."

She threw a look over her shoulder. "You don't own two kingdoms, Ty." She shook her head with a laugh. "You're a prince of both who will never be king of either."

He shrugged.

It wasn't until they were farther into the courtyard they realized something was wrong. Guards stood at each entrance to the house and stables, but they weren't all wearing uniforms of the Leroy men.

They were queen's men. Royal guards.

"Tyson," Amalie hissed. "What are your mother's men doing here?"

Someone spotted them and yelled. The guards closed in, trying to cut off any means of escape.

"Who goes there?" One called.

Amalie released the reins of her horse. It would be fine in the enclosed courtyard. "I should ask you that question. This is my house."

A guard, larger than the rest, stepped forward and removed his helmet. "By order of the crown, this estate now belongs to the kingdom. A traitor's lands are forfeit."

Amalie whipped her head around to stare at Tyson. "Did you know this?"

Betrayal stabbed through her. His mother stole what was rightfully hers. She'd seen Catrine as a mother when she'd had none.

The guard went on. "You are trespassing on royal property. We can't allow you to leave until you're questioned."

"What?" Amalie sputtered. "First you take my home and now... am I under arrest?"

Tyson stepped forward to intercede, but the guard put up a hand. "I'm sorry, your Highness." Of course, they recognized him. "This estate house is under close guard."

Amalie met the eyes of the man in Leroy colors who'd allowed her to enter. Had he known what would happen to her?

She didn't have time to consider it before two guards gripped her arms.

Tyson was slow to react as he swung a stunned gaze from the guards to Amalie. Fight for me, she wanted to yell at him.

But she knew it was futile. Tyson wouldn't use his water magic or his sword on his mother's men. She'd seen the torn loyalty in his eyes.

"My mother will hear about this."

Amalie sighed. All Tyson had left were his words. They'd been enough for her, to make her happy and keep her smiling. But they weren't enough to keep her safe. Not if his loyalty didn't completely rest with her.

All he did as they hauled her away was watch, his mouth arguing for her, but his body remaining in place.

They took her to the cells her father built to keep the village in line. He'd confined many thieves behind these bars.

Each cell was meant to house many people, but only one man sat in the corner. The guard opened the door, and Amalie stepped in, no longer fighting it. The guards at least didn't treat her roughly.

As the iron clanged shut behind her, the man on the ground tilted his face up to hers. An unkempt beard coated his cheeks, but his laughing blue eyes hadn't changed.

"John."

One side of his mouth curved up into a smile. "Hey, Ames."

A piece of her heart she hadn't known was missing fit back

into place as she let her eyes linger on his face. John Little had been her best friend and brother since the first time she escaped into the village when she was young.

She hadn't seen him in years, but meeting him in that cell was the beginning of the greatest adventure of their lives.

And she hadn't known it at the time, but it was the beginning of the end for her and Tyson.

Chapter Nine

Present

"He's waking up!" Tuck's call cut through the evening air as Amalie fastened the tie of her pants. She'd walked off for some privacy to relieve herself, thinking it would be okay to leave John for just a moment.

When she reached the wagon, Tuck knelt in the back, his face so close to John's it looked as if he was kissing him.

Amalie pulled herself up and pushed Tuck aside. John's eyelids shifted, and his lips parted as he gasped for air.

"Hey," she cooed, touching his cheek. "You're okay."

His breath calmed at her touch, but a groan rumbled in his throat. He didn't open his eyes before he spoke. "Ames?"

A tear slid down her cheek and she wiped it away. She didn't have an emotional friendship with John. Theirs was based on strength and courage.

"I'm here," she whispered.

"Why do I feel like I've had an arrow rip through me? Again." He opened his eyes and pinned her with a dark stare.

Tuck laughed and Amalie sent him a scowl before turning back to John. "You've been through a lot. Tuck has your wound wrapped, but you should try not to move too much. Your head might be a little foggy from the herb we gave you."

"Amalie Leroy," he rasped. "Why do I have another wound? And apparently, I've been drugged?"

Amalie bit back a smile. He was in pain. She shouldn't be laughing at him, but the way he stared at her in accusation, after she'd saved his life... she couldn't help it.

"You should be dead." The reality of the situation crashed over her, and her muffled laughs turned to swallowed sobs. She wouldn't break down in front of him.

His expression softened. "You save me, Ames?"

He knew very well she had, but she nodded anyway. "I will always save you. You are my family."

He tried to sit up but Amalie put a hand on his chest. "We're only a few hours from the village."

He stopped fighting her, his entire body relaxing under the weight of her words. They all knew what it meant that she'd said village instead of her estate. As soon as the guards realized John's body was missing, he'd be a wanted man. He couldn't be seen associating with Lady Leroy. But the people in the village would protect him. They may not know the identity of the Hood, but they knew everything she did for them. They were the Hood's people as much as Lady Leroy's.

"We need to get moving." Tuck placed a hand on Amalie's arm.

She nodded, giving Tuck a brief look before he climbed onto the driver's seat, and the cart lurched forward.

Exhaustion and confusion kept John quiet as Amalie held his hand. With each bump in the road, his face creased in quiet grimace. Her fault. The pain. Everything was her fault. They'd captured him because of one of her missions and almost hanged for his association with her. She should have protected him.

Blood seeped through the bandage on his shoulder, but she had no means to change it. *Hold on John,* she thought. *We're almost there.* But even her thoughts betrayed her because she knew it wasn't as easy as returning home. John had to get out of Gaule or risk being an outlaw like so many of her men who lived in the woods. It wasn't the life she wanted for him.

And then there was Tyson, on his way to the last place the Hood was seen. The same village they neared now.

Darkness still shrouded the world as they approached the mass of huddled buildings. They stopped right outside the village near the Leroy estate and Tuck turned to her.

"You can't be seen with him." He jerked his head to John who'd fallen asleep.

"What about you?"

"I have to risk it."

She saw the wisdom behind his words, but leaving John didn't feel right. Finally, she breathed a sigh and heaved herself up, jumping from the wagon bed. "I'll fetch Maiya."

She trudged through the streets, John heavy on her mind. Wanted posters lined alleyways. Her face and the faces of some of her men held so much more depth than they showed. They couldn't be reduced down to a single crime. They weren't only worth what others thought they did wrong. She released a sigh, resisting the urge to tear the posters down as she kept walking.

Cameron stood guard at the gate. He recognized her immediately and rushed forward.

"You're alive," he said, stating the obvious with a grunt as he looked her over.

"Cam, we don't have time. I need Maiya."

Cam nodded and ushered them through the small door.

The larger gates had remained closed since the day she forced the royal guards from the grounds. Amalie ran up the steps and into the hall, winding her way through the long corridors until she reached Maiya's room. Three short knocks brought the heavy-lidded girl to her door.

One look at Amalie's face wiped the sleep from Maiya's expression. "John?" she asked.

"In the village. He needs you." She nodded, pausing only to change from her sleeping gown into loose fitting linen pants and silk shirt.

Amalie didn't need to say where in the village Tuck had taken John. The town blacksmith had a room behind his shop he reserved for the Hood's business. Many of her men couldn't show their faces in the middle of the city, but they were injured frequently, and Maiya healed them there.

John was now just another one of her hidden people. Another man condemned by the crown for crimes he had no choice but to commit.

"How have things been in my absence?" Amalie lifted her tired eyes to Cam's. One of her most trusted guards, he was always honest with her in a way few others were. "Have the men behaved themselves?"

"For the most part." His jaw clenched and Amalie waited for him to say the words she could see behind his troubled eyes. "We had a visitor while you were away."

She sighed. Nothing good ever came from visitors. They only brought with them pain and suspicion. "Which of the queen's men did she send?"

That could be the only explanation for the troubled expression on Cam's face. They all knew the queen would do everything in her power to find Simon. Until then, Amalie had been too consumed with her journey and the need to save John to consider what came next. Simon knew who she was, and she didn't know what to do with him yet.

Darkness clouded Cam's eyes as he spit out a name. "Anders."

Surprise surged through Amalie. Edmund's father was one of the queen's most loyal captains. If she sent him, it was only a matter of time before they discovered the truth. Anders had never taken a liking to Amalie because of her closeness with the princes. He loved the queen, but not her sons. Or his own son for that matter. Like many Gauleans, Anders continued to see magic as a scourge, rather than the blessing that erased La Dame from their lives.

Amalie rubbed the stiffness from her neck. Riding did torture on her body. "What does Anders suspect of us?"

Cam glanced from right to left, making sure they wouldn't be overheard. "He didn't connect you to the hood, but Simon disappeared from your lands. There were accusations in his words. He doesn't suspect you of wearing the disguise yourself, but he thinks this estate harbors the man."

Amalie's heart pounded inside her chest. He was too close. If she knew Anders at all, she knew he wouldn't give up. She took a step back. "Why would he think such a thing?" Had she made some mistake? Revealed her true feelings about the Hood's mission?

Cam pinned her with a stare. "You've never hidden your feelings about the nobility. It isn't a far stretch to think the Leroy estate took some pleasure in food meant for the rich going to the poor instead."

Amalie's shoulders relaxed. Cam was right. All Anders had on her was her willingness to help the poor and the fact that the Hood operated on her lands. She'd made sure to also steal shipments on the lands of her neighboring nobles, but it wasn't enough.

"Will he be back?" she asked, already knowing the answer. Anders would insist on speaking with her.

Cam nodded. "He said he'd return after a journey to the young Duke Caron's estate."

"Duke Caron?" She didn't know the duke, but she'd known his father when he was a constant presence at the palace. That wasn't what concerned her in that moment though. A village on the edge of the Caron lands, at the northern edge of the Gaulean border, held the biggest secret of her life. Tucked away in a suffering village was the biggest sacrifice she'd made as the Hood. If Anders discovered everything she'd given up, her entire life as the Hood would come crashing down around her.

No one could know what existed in that town. Not only would the Hood be finished, but a life would be in danger.

Amalie hardened her jaw. She wouldn't let this break her, make her feel. Emotions were a weakness she couldn't afford.

"You can return to your post, Cameron. Tuck and Maiya should return soon so watch for them. I'm going to see our guest before retiring for the night."

He nodded once and left.

Amalie walked to the room she'd given Simon in while she was gone. Four guards stood outside his door. Simon was a magic man. His power was an added strength, but he still had limitations and wasn't strong enough to best four other men at once.

He was still human after all. She'd counted on his acknowledging that fact and not attempting escape.

"Report," she said as she stepped up beside one of the guards.

He didn't hesitate. "The prisoner has eaten everything we've brought."

"How has his demeanor been?"

"We've barely heard anything from him."

That wasn't a surprise. She knew Simon. He wasn't one to treat people poorly even while they held him captive.

Amalie glanced to the guard once more. "Don't call him a prisoner." She took an offered key and unlocked the door, pushing it open before closing it behind her.

Despite the late hour, he sat in front of the dwindling fire, a glow dancing across his chiseled face.

"Amalie." He lifted a cup of tea to his lips, not turning to her. "Welcome back."

She eyed the tray of china cups with a pot of tea in the center, relief striking her. Her people treated him well. That was something at least.

Practically collapsing into an oversized chair, she sighed. Like Catrine, Simon had always been kind to her. But she'd never forgive the crown for trying to take her home or forsaking the people of the kingdom.

Simon studied her over the rim of his cup. "I overheard the guards speak of Captain Anders' visit."

She'd already pushed the captain from her mind. He was a problem for a new day. Finally, the words she'd wanted to say tumbled out of her. "Tyson's coming here."

Simon raised an eyebrow. He was one of the few people who knew everything she'd been through with Ty. Well, not everything. But Simon was the only person they'd told of their impulsive decision all those years ago. Still, he waited for her to explain.

"He's been sent to find you."

Simon nodded as if he'd expected that all along. "Tell me, Amalie, does your husband know of your secret identity?"

No, she thought. But he didn't deserve her secrets. Not anymore.

Chapter Ten

Three years ago

Tyson froze. When it was time to fight for the woman he loved, he couldn't do it. He couldn't go against his mother.

Tyson had seen it in her eyes. The knowledge that some part of him might never be hers.

He'd seen things in Dracon he'd never imagined. So much death. He'd almost lost everyone he loved. At the end of the fight, his sword was bathed in blood and his soul was forever tarnished. He'd almost given his life to protect everyone he loved. His mother. Etta. Alex. Edmund. How could he give every bit of his loyalty to only one person after everything they'd all been through?

He had to figure out a way. Amalie deserved every part of him.

The guards who'd taken Amalie away offered him a suite of rooms once belonging to Amalie's father.

Because he was the prince, and she was the daughter of a trai-

tor. He'd sent word to his mother and then spent days sitting idly by as they'd questioned Amalie. What more could he do? The guards wouldn't allow him to see her.

Soon, they'd realized she was no threat and released her. But what of her estate? Until recently, she'd refused to return, stating she didn't want lands that were so tainted. But then word had come from the village. A friend of hers had disappeared.

Tyson didn't know the friend, but he knew he'd do anything to wipe the worry from her eyes. To make her smile, as carefree as she'd been only a week ago when they'd decided their futures and tied themselves together.

He smiled at the memory, lost in his own mind until the clop of a horse's hooves entered the courtyard. Tyson jumped up from his spot near the steps as soon as he recognized the man sliding down from the beast.

If his mother had sent Simon, it must mean Amalie would be okay.

Tyson ran forward, stopping himself from throwing his arms around the other man in relief.

"My prince." Simon dipped his head. He'd always insisted on formality between him and the royal family.

"Si, they're keeping Amalie in a cell."

"I know." He handed his horse's reins to a stable lad and marched toward the line of guards near the front entryway. "We will fix this, your Highness. Show me to the captain."

Tyson led Simon inside and to the room he'd spend most of his time in recently. He couldn't count the number of times he'd pleaded for her release. Treason tarnished the names of entire families in Gaule. Amalie would never be free of it. There would always be suspicion.

The captain looked up from his desk as they barged through the door. He straightened immediately upon seeing Simon. "Sir, what brings you so far from the palace?"

Simon let the charged air linger in silence for a moment before answering. "You're imprisoning a young woman who has done no wrong."

The captain's jaw tensed and he narrowed his eyes. "The traitor's daughter refused to leave the queen's property."

Anger burned in Tyson. "You arrested her before she even had a chance to refuse."

He wanted to unleash his magic, showering the captain in a torrent of water, but the power stopped at his fingertips, fighting the urge to break free as it had every day since the battle.

And Tyson hated himself for it. He hated that he couldn't bring himself to do what was necessary to protect the woman he loved. He despised himself for being weak, for letting the battle steal the fight from his soul.

Simon remained calm as ever. "Amalie Leroy is not her father. The queen regards her highly."

Tyson averted his eyes, not wanting to dwell on the thoughts rising to the surface. If his mother loved Amalie so much, why did she seize the Leroy estate?

The captain scoffed. "That girl and her family no longer deserve to hold a title in Gaule."

Simon crossed his arms. "By order of the queen, I demand you release her." He jerked his head to the door. "Go. I'll wait here."

For a minute, Tyson thought the guard would refuse, but he only shook his head and left them.

Tyson collapsed into a chair in front of the desk.

Simon put a hand on his shoulder and squeezed. "It's good you sent for me."

Tyson leaned forward to put his head in his hands. What was wrong with him? All he could do for Amalie was send for help.

"I'm the prince, Si. I should have been able to get her released." But he knew the truth. The captain may not have arrested him because he was the queen's son, but he was also a magic man, not trusted or obeyed. The last few days had been full of suspicious looks and lack of conversation. They didn't want him there.

Maybe Gaule was no longer his home. He shook his head. Amalie was in Gaule and he'd go wherever she was.

"I tried to get her to come with me to Bela," Tyson admitted. "But she said it was time to right her father's wrongs and take care of the people living on Leroy lands."

Simon studied him for a long moment. "You care for her a great deal."

A laugh bubbled up from his chest. "Yes, I care for her." He lifted his face, meeting Simon's gaze. "She's my wife."

Present

Wife. It used to seem like such a big word to Tyson until the day he married Amalie in a small village near the Caron estate with only strangers as witnesses. A friar performed the ceremony, a young man named Tuck who'd befriended them both.

They'd thought the future lay open before them, theirs for the taking.

Within a year, everything fell apart. Tyson still didn't know why they hadn't told his family of their happiness. Maybe they'd thought it wouldn't last once they shared their secret with the world.

Well, they'd only ever told one man, and it still faded like the autumn sun, bright one day and cloudy the next.

He didn't know why Simon hadn't told his mother, but he supposed it didn't matter. He only knew he was grateful and that he now had to be there for the guard who'd always been there for him. He had to fight for him.

For the past two years, he'd heard the comments from those he lived with in Bela, never recovering the man he once was. Etta and Alex's constant worry exhausted him, but he couldn't bring himself to take joy in the life around him.

Not when he was so broken. Not when something vital was missing inside him.

Edmund stood beside him, staring at the walls of the Leroy estate. If there was anyone who understood how he felt, it was the blonde warrior. He'd spent months thinking Estevan was dead.

"Are you sure we have to do this?" Edmund asked, glancing sideways.

No, Tyson wanted to say. They could stay at an inn in the village as they searched for any information on the Hood. But he'd never been able to help himself when he had the opportunity to see Amalie, no matter how cold her welcome was.

"I..." He blew out a breath. This was Edmund, a man as close to Tyson as his own brother. They'd been through a lot together and he trusted him with his life. The secrets he carried in his heart threatened to blow it to pieces one final time.

He closed his eyes. "There's something I never told you, Edmund." His eyes slid open to view the structure that had always had an ominous air around it. "Amalie and I... we got married."

Edmund's eyes widened in shock, but his lips tilted into a smile. "Oh."

"Oh? That's all you have to say?"

His grin widened. "I'm not sure why you never told us... but it's kind of funny, you have to admit."

"Why is it funny?" He crossed his arms over his chest.

Edmund chuckled. "Amalie Leroy, the lady who has gained

a reputation for despising her fellow nobles and forsaking the queen is a princess of both Gaule and Bela."

The irony wasn't lost on Tyson, but he didn't get a chance to respond as a guard approached them.

"Back away from the wall," he commanded.

Tyson sighed. "Tell Lady Amalie that Tyson has arrived." Amalie had to have known they were coming and knowing her she was prepared.

The guard disappeared through a door in the wall, appearing a few moments later. "Come with me."

He led them into the courtyard and gestured for a stable boy to take their horses. "Lady Amalie has retired for the night. I will show you to the guest wing and she'll see you after first light."

Something in Tyson's chest deflated, and his nerves calmed. He'd both wanted to see her and dreaded it.

Edmund gripped his shoulder and laughed once more before stepping into the first room they were offered.

The guard gestured for Tyson to follow him to another room. Nothing had changed in the Leroy estate. Sparse furnishings sat in barely decorated rooms. No luxuries were afforded the residents of this house. Amalie spent all of her land's earnings making life better for the people who relied on her.

It was one of the things he loved best about her. She cared in a way few people did. In a different life, a different world, they could have been happy together.

He jumped when the door slammed behind him, shutting him in the silence of his mind. He'd experienced many stages of loneliness over the last two years, trying to forget the emptiness inside him with missions into foreign kingdoms and duties for his mother and sister. When one belonged to two kingdoms, it was almost like they belonged to neither.

He wasn't truly Gaulean or wholly Belaen. For a while,

Amalie understood what it felt like to be a stranger in one's own home. But she'd found her place. He never had.

He toed off his boots and loosened his sword belt to let it drop to the floor. Stripping off his travel clothes as he walked, he made it to the edge of the bed before collapsing into it and letting himself dream of a time when life had seemed so damned easy.

A THROAT CLEARING woke Tyson as the sun streamed through the window, casting shadows on the floor.

The throat cleared again, and the hairs on his arms stood on end. He could feel her presence before setting eyes on her delicate face.

"You shouldn't be here, Tyson." Amalie's voice cracked on his name.

He groaned as he rolled onto his side to face her. She sat in a chair across the room, one leg crossed over the other. Her hard eyes betrayed her calm countenance.

The fabric of her pale blue dress bunched at her waist, and she smoothed it out. Her silken hair billowed as a breeze filtered in through the window, chilling the air.

She stood and crossed the room to shut the thin pane of glass, her movements stiff.

Shaking himself out of his momentary stupor, Tyson spoke. "You knew I was coming, Ames."

She closed her eyes. "Don't call me that. Please."

He sighed. "Amalie, I have orders to seek the Hood and find the queen's guard he's taken prisoner."

A flicker of emotion he couldn't decipher crossed her face. "You are a guest in my house, and I won't turn you away, but the information you seek will not be here. Just ask Captain Anders.

He's already interrogated my people when I wasn't here. You'd do better seeking a bed in the village."

"Ames," he breathed. "Can we be civil for one moment?"

"I was being civil." She crossed her arms, refusing to look at him.

Tyson wanted one look, one moment when he could try to read her like he'd done so well in the past, but she gave him nothing. He nodded, realizing he wouldn't get anywhere with her. He'd never understood her vitriol toward him when she'd been the one to break them. "Okay then. You've come this morning to let me know I am unwelcome here. Message received. I see no need for us to suffer one another's presence any longer. I will risk staying in the village." He pushed the blanket off him, not caring about his state of undress.

Amalie looked away.

Tyson stood and pulled his pants on. "I don't know what I was thinking." He paused, turning to her as she refused to meet his eyes. He'd known how she'd treat him when he arrived, yet he came anyway.

Where was the girl he'd once known?

He walked past her, still shirtless. "This was a mistake. I'll inform Edmund to seek us accommodation elsewhere."

She opened her mouth to speak, but before the words were out, the door opened, revealing a smiling Edmund.

"Morning prince." Edmund glanced from Tyson to Amalie. "And princess."

Tyson froze. He should have known Edmund would make a big deal of his revelation.

Amalie turned on him. "You told him?" The accusation in her voice stung.

Tyson only shrugged.

She huffed out a breath, looking as if she had more to say

until she met Edmund's gaze. Something passed between them, unspoken words, and Amalie stepped back.

Tyson didn't understand what was going on.

Amalie gritted her teeth. "I am not a princess."

Edmund hadn't stopped grinning. "On the contrary, my dear, the law says you are. And you're like a double princess since your husband here has two kingdoms to call his own."

Tyson winced at the term husband. "Edmund, let it go. We're leaving. There should be a few open rooms in one of the inns."

He picked up his discarded shirt and sword before stepping in to the hall. Footsteps followed him and he assumed it was Edmund until Amalie's voice called him back.

"Tyson, wait." She ran to catch up with him, her cheeks flushed as he'd seen so many times before.

He slung his shirt over one shoulder and turned. "What is it, Amalie? Do you have to get one final word in before I leave? I didn't come here for you, but I won't lie and say you hadn't crossed my mind. It was a mistake and one I won't make again. This is the last time I will bother you. You have my word."

Insecurity crossed her face, revealing some of the girl he'd once loved. "You can stay."

"But you said—"

"I know very well what I said. And my mind has altered. Edmund is always welcome in my home."

"And me?"

"You?" She ran a hand through her long chestnut curls.

"Last time I was here with Helena and Dell there was ice between us. I don't want my presence to cause us both pain."

"You don't cause me pain, Tyson." Her voice softened, but her next words were the worst of all. "Everything between us is in the past. The world continues to turn, and we must move on with our lives."

He looked into the eyes of the woman he'd once pledged his life to and saw nothing but cold acceptance in their depths. She truly had moved beyond the love that continued to consume him. He didn't know what he'd expected, but it hadn't been that.

He rubbed the back of his neck. "Okay. We'll stay." It was all he could do to not leave the estate behind and never return.

But the only thing worse than seeing Amalie and not being able to hold her would have been never seeing her at all.

Chapter Eleven

Tyson's mother sent him to hunt down criminals in Gaule before. He'd spent the years since the war with Dracon doing his mother's bidding as well as his sister's. It was never easy serving two queens, but he loved them both.

Edmund remained suspiciously quiet as they left the home of another person who refused to give them the information they wanted, stating they'd told everything they knew to the guard who'd come before.

Tyson hated that Anders had been there before him. He tried to imagine the captain gently asking these people the questions he had, but there was nothing gentle about the man. One of the estate guards told him Anders planned to return soon, and Tyson wanted to be long gone before then. He hadn't yet told Edmund of his father's involvement, but suspected that wouldn't go over well. Edmund had no love for the man who'd raised him and now despised him for his magic.

Tyson's mind ran through the possibilities and scenarios

that might lead them closer to their target. Each thought that struck him came out in a jumble of words.

He sidestepped a young boy who was lying against the nearest building, huddled in a threadbare blanket. One naked foot stuck out into the chilly air. He wasn't the first beggar they'd come across, but he was only a child. The boy stared up at Tyson with wide, all-seeing eyes. There was an innocence in them that would be taken with a few more winters on the streets.

Tyson paused and crouched down to peer into the boy's dirty face, an idea striking him. The people of the village only watched him with thinly veiled hostility and suspicion. They spoke in short sentences, choosing their words carefully.

All Tyson had learned was the Hood was a revered figure in these parts rather than the villain the guardsmen painted him as, the criminal who abducted Simon. It was time he learned the truth.

"Hello." He offered the boy a smile. "What's your name?"

Indecision flashed in the boy's eyes, but he lifted his chin. "Arthur, your Highness." Tyson should have been shocked the kid knew who he was, but word traveled fast in the villages.

"Well, Arthur, you look hungry. Would you like to come to the tavern with me and my friend here?"

Arthur's eyes widened, and he licked his cracked lips before nodding. Tyson helped him to his feet. The blanket fell to the ground, but he didn't bend to retrieve it. Instead, Tyson unfastened his own cloak and set it around the boy's shoulders. Arthur tensed for a moment before wrapping the cloak tighter around him.

Tyson wondered for a moment where the kid's parents were, but some things were better left unasked.

Arthur walked in front of them, leading the way to the tavern. Edmund pulled Tyson back. "Where is this going?"

Tyson shrugged off his hand. "The boy needed some kindness."

Edmund shook his head. "We passed many people in the same condition. Why choose him?"

Tyson couldn't explain the way he'd felt drawn to Arthur as if he had everything the prince was looking for. He didn't know how to say he'd seen some of himself, his hopelessness, reflected in the eyes of a beggar. Tyson was a prince. He should have everything. And for years, he'd felt as if he had nothing.

Darkness clouded his life. If he couldn't help himself, he could help the young boy. He could help Simon.

As the door of the tavern open, raucous laughter spilled out. They stepped through and all sound died except the scrape of their boots against the stone floor. Suspicion choked the air. Tyson tried to ignore the looks sent his way. It wasn't the first time he'd experienced this in the same village. They had no love for their royal family, and Tyson only represented everything they hated.

Not only was he a known magic man, but he was also a Durand.

Arthur, seeming not to notice, led them to an empty table in the corner. Edmund tensed beside Tyson and rested his hand on the hilt of his sword, a clear threat.

Tyson sighed. That was sure to win the villagers trust. He waved a hand to Edmund, telling him to relax, and strode to where Arthur sat with an expectant look on his face. Chatter resumed, the jovial aura from before a distant memory.

Relaxing in the wooden booth, Tyson ran a hand over the top of his head. How had his mother allowed the kingdom to sink into such a state where her son's presence turned a village into a viper's nest? Was this only because of Anders' visit the week before, or did the resentment run deeper than that?

Had she known? Part of him wanted to believe there was

nothing she could do to stem the tide of hatred. His father—or at least the man he'd always thought was his father—kept strict control over his guardsmen through fear and brutality. His mother attempted kindness, and they responded by becoming an undisciplined force that terrorized the people they were meant to protect.

It wasn't the queen who led these people down this path, but the people sworn to serve her.

He thought back on a time soon after the battle with Dracon when they seized the Leroy estate. It was true it had been the law that a traitor's lands were forfeit, but that hadn't made it right.

And Simon had stood by his side, allowing him to work through every internal difficulty. He'd been a friend that day.

Tyson narrowed his eyes and leaned forward to face Arthur. He hated himself for what he had to do, but it was for Simon.

Arthur darted his eyes away, fixing them on a serving girl ambling their way.

"What can I get you?" She didn't meet their eyes as she twirled a curl around her finger.

Edmund was the one who spoke. "Three ciders, bread, and some of whatever you have on the spit."

She walked away without another word.

"Arthur," Tyson began. "You'd like to fill your belly, wouldn't you?"

Arthur nodded vigorously.

"You can have whatever you want, boy... as long as I get the information I seek."

Arthur bit the inside of his cheek and fixed his eyes on the table. "I know nothing, sir. I swear it."

"Nothing about what?"

"I heard you was looking for the Hood. Everyone in town knows that. Just like that man before."

Tyson drummed his fingers against the table, ignoring the man before comment. "Why are people here protecting a criminal?"

Arthur finally lifted his eyes, fire blazing in their depths. "The Hood ain't no criminal. You come here and feed me for a day expecting me to betray the one who feeds me all my other days."

Tyson pursed his lips as the serving girl returned, practically throwing four wooden plates onto the table. A foul-smelling meat sat in front of them, turning Tyson's stomach.

Arthur, however, eyed the food like the starving boy he was. Tyson slid the plate out of his reach.

"You speak of betraying the Hood, but that man betrays the kingdom with every action."

A hand landed on Tyson's shoulder. "Don't answer him, Arthur." A man slid into the long booth and pushed a plate toward the boy. Arthur didn't hesitate in availing himself of the offered meat.

"What are you doing here, Tuck?" Tyson growled. He hadn't seen his friend in two years.

"You know this guy?" Edmund asked. "He was at the palace."

"I used to."

"Used to?" Tuck laughed, his large frame shaking. "I married the bastard to Lady Amalie. Tell me, Ty, how did you instill such venom in one so small?"

Tyson ignored the comment because he'd wondered the same thing many times. "I didn't know you'd come to these parts." He flicked his eyes to Arthur who'd practically licked his plate clean. "And you've obviously been here a while."

Tuck shrugged. "I came about a year ago and realized this village needed me more than I needed to maintain my traveling ways. Amalie needed me."

Tyson bristled at that. "Well, as you can see we're busy so our reunion will have to wait."

Tuck slid an arm over Arthur's shoulders. "The problem, Prince, is that I can't let you question Arthur here. The boy deserves better than the traitor stamp he'll receive if he tells you what you seek."

"He's already a traitor for protecting a man wanted by the crown."

Humor sparked in Tuck's eyes. "Yes, we can't have anyone protecting wanted... men." He scratched his chin. "I'll tell you what... release the boy and I'll tell you what you want to know. But only you." He looked to Edmund. "You must send your body guard back to the estate."

"I don't need body guards," Tyson grumbled.

"Right." Tuck waved his fingers through the air. "Because you have powers."

Tyson scowled. "Fine. Edmund, go back to the estate. I'll be okay with Tuck."

"You sure you can trust this guy?" Edmund narrowed his eyes.

"Yes." Tyson's shoulders sagged. He'd known the moment he met Tuck in that broken village he was a good man. When he'd convinced his family to open rooms at their inn to two travelers who refused to divulge their names at first, he'd become a friend.

And then when he tied them together, he'd become a part of their lives, forever cemented into their memories. As Edmund led Arthur away, Tyson studied his old friend. Sitting across from him brought all the memories he'd tried to keep buried to the forefront of his mind.

The harsh lines of Tuck's face relaxed. "It's good to see you, Ty."

Emotion thickened in Tyson's throat and he cleared it away. "It really is."

"I was sorry to miss you at the palace a few weeks ago, but Amalie needed me."

Tyson didn't show his surprise that Tuck had been there. "I'm sorry about her friend." And he was. Even if John Little had been an agent of the Hood's, he'd meant something to Amalie and he'd be forever sorry for any pain she felt.

Now that Tuck sat in front of him, he couldn't focus on the mission he'd been set on. "How is she, Tuck?"

Tuck smiled in sympathy. "Good. I think. Amalie isn't one to allow any of us to see into her mind. After... everything between you two happened, I came here with her and haven't left her side."

"I'm glad she has people around who care about her." He'd been worried about that since the day she forced him to leave. Amalie no longer had any family.

Tuck dipped his head to meet Tyson's gaze, something unspoken in his eyes. "We're taking care of her."

Tyson laughed. "She'd say she doesn't need taken care of."

"And she'd be right." He tilted his head. "She never told me why you left... or why you didn't come back."

The mystery of what happened had haunted Tyson every minute of every day for the last two years. One minute, he'd been inescapably in love and the next, he was in mourning for what he'd lost. Something died that day and at times, he wished it had been him.

Tyson coughed and reached for his untouched cider. Taking a sip, he closed his eyes for the briefest of moments.

Tuck, maybe sensing he wasn't going to get the story, asked a question that was more like a statement. "You still love her?"

Tyson set his cup down. "Amalie... shit, yes. I never stopped. She's the most infuriating person I've ever known, but for the last two years, she's stolen my every thought." He rubbed the back of his neck. "I wasn't going to come back here again. I was going to try moving on with my life. But the man who is missing... he's a friend. I'll do anything to get him back, even if it means stirring up old feelings better left buried."

Tuck considered his words for a moment before nodding. "You aren't going to find what you're searching for in the village. They all owe the Hood too much. Frankly, I do too, but I don't want you harassing innocent boys like Arthur."

Tyson only heard part of what he'd said because his mind stuck on only a few of the words. "You know who the Hood is."

"If I say yes, are you going to arrest me?" He slid out of the booth. "Come with me."

They walked across the tavern and stepped out into the chilly air. Finally, Tyson could breathe again.

Tuck started walking. "I'm not going to give up the Hood, but I do want to show you something."

Tyson cursed. "Why is everyone protecting a thief?"

"That's what I wanted to show you. This village has long felt abandoned by the crown. Then the Hood came and showed them someone still cared, someone saw their plight."

"You're trying to tell me that a man who attacks caravans and traders is noble?"

"I'm only going to show you why this village needs help and let you come to your own conclusions."

Tyson didn't say another word until they'd reached the market district. Empty shops showed no signs of use. Cracked stone roads and crumbling buildings surrounded the square.

Tuck walked through the center. "Three years ago, Duke Leroy let his guard descend on the town to force all able-bodied men to join him in his rebellion against the crown. They had no choice but were painted as traitors, anyway. Traders avoided the village, taking their goods on roads just outside of town. The crown ceased providing extra food stores." He turned into an alleyway that led down a road between two hills. A large tree sat atop one, its branches reaching toward the sky.

Tuck pointed to it. "That's where Lord Leroy's men hung anyone suspected of magic."

Tyson had heard the story from Etta. She'd traveled to the Leroy estate to protect the magic folk, arresting the Duke and delivering him to the palace. Standing where it happened had a sobering effect, but it didn't change his mission.

Find the Hood. Save Simon. Bring the Hood to the queen. Return home to Bela where he could once again try to forget the girl who'd made him leave her behind.

Nothing in that plan left any room to feel sympathy for a man who was nothing more than a criminal. He turned away from the tree on the hill.

Tuck sighed. "They needed hope, Tyson. Surely you can see that after everything your people went through."

His people. The magic folk. The ones who weren't welcome on this side of the border.

He clenched his jaw. "Tuck, I appreciate what you're trying to do, but I am a prince. My first loyalty is to my mother. You say the Hood is some noble man, but he has abducted the noblest man I know." He took a step back down the alley and paused. "I'm sorry. I have a job to do."

Tuck didn't follow him back across the abandoned market square. Exhaustion weighed on Tyson's mind as he tried to put the pieces into place. He couldn't count the number of people he'd questioned, and he was no closer to finding this man who was supposedly a figure of hope.

This village had suffered. That much was clear. It hurt to see any part of the kingdom he'd once called his own fall on such hard times, but it wasn't his problem. After he found the Hood, he'd once again leave Gaule behind.

At least he told himself those things.

In truth, he wished there was more he could do.

He entered the darkened space between two buildings, just wanting to get back to the Estate house and sink into his bed.

A noise behind him made him freeze. The scuff of boots running toward him. He didn't even have time to yell before a sack was thrown over his head and his head hit something hard, sending his already dark world into blackness.

Chapter Twelve

Amalie sat on a wooden bench in the courtyard watching a few of her men train with swords. The clang of metal swirled in the air and she soaked in the sounds. She'd always loved the feel of an estate at work. As a girl, she'd made a habit of escaping her tutors to watch her father's men battle each other. She'd only picked up a sword a few times growing up, and it wasn't until she'd reclaimed her father's estate that John trained her with a bow.

Thinking of that time sent a stab of pain through her chest. She'd lied to Tyson. Her life had changed so drastically in the past years, but moving on from him had proven impossible.

She didn't know why she treated him so poorly. In his presence, her anger gained the best of her.

Someone dropped onto the seat beside her, and she peered at Maiya out of the corner of her eye.

"I've heard talk," Maiya began. "Tyson and Edmund have been questioning the villagers. After Anders and his men tore through town, they don't look kindly on another inquisition."

Amalie glanced around to make sure they were not over-heard. The guards she hired were part of her hidden life, but most of the servants were unaware of how their mistress spent her nights. On top of that, having houseguests made her nervous.

Tyson had come in search of Simon. What would he do if he found the queen's man in her home?

Amalie pursed her lips as she took in the girl's muddy boots before reaching out to pull a leaf from her unkempt ebony curls. She raised an eyebrow. "You were in the woods today?"

Maiya only shrugged in answer. She had a habit of seeking solitude wherever she could find it, but the woods behind the estate weren't her usual place of contemplation. For travelers, they were dangerous. Some of the Merry Men wanted by the crown had set up a homestead among the trees.

Amalie nodded in understanding. She'd lived most of her life in grand houses or the palace, but this girl had spent her years among simple village folk in the peace of her father's healing shop.

"Have any of the villagers been harassing the prince?" She didn't want the queen's guard to be called to protect Tyson. That wouldn't end well for her people.

Maiya shook her head. "They've been trying to keep their distance, but he's persistent. John doesn't think he'll ever give up."

Amalie turned to her. "You saw John?" Her friend had been a constant weight on her mind. She'd been unable to see him since Maiya healed his wound, but Tuck had kept her apprised of his situation. He'd joined some of her other men in their forest dwellings.

Maiya lowered her gaze. "That's why I went to the woods. I wanted to check on him. When I healed him... there was a moment I thought I was too late."

Amalie reached for Maiya's hand and squeezed. "Thank you for saving him."

She still didn't raise her eyes. "He sent me with a message for you. Stop sending Tuck to him with supplies. He worries with the prince at the estate, someone will connect you to him."

Amalie had considered the same thing, but she'd refused to leave John to his own devices. "What else?"

"A few of the men have returned from a village nearer to the palace. They speak of raids. The royal guard has been harassing villagers in search of the Hood and her associates. It won't be long before they reach our village."

Amalie sucked in a breath. She knew it would be a possibility as soon as they arrested John. Soon, single arrests wouldn't be enough for Catrine.

Amalie had waited for more units of the royal guard to come, but Catrine only sent Anders' men and Tyson. Why?

"Did John say how long we have?"

Maiya shook her head. "No, but he knows how to get the information."

She didn't like where this was headed. "Just say it, Maiya."

"They're going to extract it from the prince." She said it as if it was the most obvious thing in the world. As if the words didn't send a chill down Amalie's spine.

Her people would do anything for her, and that was what scared her the most. She needed to get to Tyson.

"Fetch my horse," she said, jumping to her feet, fear making her pulse leap in her throat.

"Amalie." Maiya held her back. "What can you do? We both know John doesn't operate like the rest of the men. He won't listen to you."

"I can't let him..." A quiver ran through her. "It's Tyson." And John. She loved her friend, but if anything happened to Ty, she'd never forgive herself. She'd never admitted it to anyone, but he was the reason she accepted the missions of the Hood. Tyson was pure, good. She'd never deserved him as the daughter of a traitor. But in trying to do the right thing, trying to clear the darkness from her soul, she'd lost him, anyway.

Maiya sighed and took off toward the stables.

It wasn't Maiya who returned leading two horses, but Tuck. He took one look at her and gestured to the beast.

"Maiya told me everything. We need to get to the village." He shook his head. "I was only with Tyson a few hours ago. I shouldn't have left him on his own."

"It's not your fault, Tuck." Amalie had never been more grateful for her friend. He'd once been a friend of Tyson's as well. Tuck was the one person who knew what Ty had really meant to her. He'd been there on the best day of her life performing the ceremony.

Amalie ordered a guard to open the gates. As soon as a wide enough gap appeared, she nudged her horse's flanks and took off into the village. There was only one place they'd take Tyson.

Two men lingered outside the blacksmith's shop so Amalie and Tuck turned down an alleyway away from prying eyes and jumped down, leaving their horses tied to a post before slipping through a back door.

The sharp trill of a hammer on steel provided a steady beat in time with the pounding of her heart. She wished she could believe John wouldn't hurt Ty, but she knew better. When it came to protecting everything they stood for, John would hold nothing back. He had even less regard for royalty than she did.

Dim light greeted them, a candle burning low, but the room was empty. Panic threatened to swallow her whole. When Tuck grabbed her arm, she jumped.

"John wouldn't do anything he can't take back."

She turned to face him. "We both know the falseness in your words, Tuck. John and some of the others don't have the same morality as you and I. If there is a raid planned, Tyson isn't safe."

She put her hands on her head. "This is my fault. I should never have let him stay. He doesn't belong in this. Tyson has always been too good for the world of criminals and thieves."

She tried to remember John as he once was, kind and calm before the world beat him down. She loved him like family, but it didn't mean she was blind to the darkness in his eyes. It had been there since she was first reunited with him as prisoners.

And now, as a wanted man, he had nothing left to lose.

Her heart clenched painfully. "We need to find them."

Chapter
Thirteen

Three Years Ago

Amalie was no longer a prisoner, but she couldn't rid herself of John's words. He'd sat in that cell as if none of it bothered him. Simon left, taking most of the queen's guard with him. Only a few guards remained. They allowed Amalie Leroy to live in the house once belonging to her family, but it was no longer hers. That much was clear.

Tyson's chest rose and fell steadily beside her. He was so close yet so far away. Her arrest put a distance between them that hadn't been there before.

The village needed a warrior, John had said. Someone with good intentions and an even better aim.

She rolled over and away from Ty. The queen, Ty's own mother, had taken the only thing that belonged to Amalie. Her estate. And she'd ignored the village beyond those walls. Amalie climbed from the bed and paced across the cold stone floor, weighing the decision in her mind.

The people needed John. With a final glance at Tyson, she pulled on a cloak over her silk sleeping gown and drew the hood up over her hair.

There was no time left for indecision. Two weeks had passed since her imprisonment and each day felt as stifling as the one before. She stepped from the room and walked toward the stairs that would take her to the lower level.

The lone guard outside the cells was one she'd heard laughing about the traitorous villagers getting what they deserved. Her father forced them into a situation that now meant the crown would not come to their aid. They'd marched to the gates of the palace, ready to fight because they'd had no other choice. They didn't get to decide if they'd betray their king, yet they were labeled traitors all the same.

If he wasn't already dead, she'd have turned her father in herself.

She crept in the shadows readying herself to make the jump Etta had taught her. When a man is bigger than you, incapacitate him before he knows you're there. And don't let him see your face.

She stood on the bottom step, judging the distance. Releasing a shuddering breath, she bent her knees and launched herself at the man, driving him sideways into a wall. Flattening her palm against the back of his head, she slammed it sideways into the stone. He collapsed to the ground, and she landed on top of him.

Rolling off, she unclipped the keys from his belt and ran toward the cells.

John must have heard the commotion because he was already on his feet. She unlocked his cell. He didn't speak as he gave her a quick hug.

Before she could stop him, he crouched beside the guard, drew the other man's knife, and slid it across his throat.

Revulsion rolled through Amalie. "What are you doing?" she hissed.

"Do you want your estate back?"

"The queen will just send more of them."

He shook his head. "I overheard this one say she no longer cared about the Leroy lands. That she didn't have the stomach to keep them."

Amalie hugged her arms over her chest as she watched the candlelight flicker across the guard's crimson blood. The John she'd known as a child wouldn't have the ability to end a man's life without even a flicker of emotion.

"Come on." He tugged her arm.

Each guard they met faced a similar end. John cut through them with precision and coldness until each of the guards were only a symbol of what the queen did to her. A carcass of trust now broken.

The Leroy men on guard held no regard for the queen's men and left them to their fates, disappearing into the barracks to avoid the deadly assassin in their midst.

John left as he'd come, the ghost of a future that scared Amalie. Before he left, he made her promise to meet him in the woods two days hence. She'd agreed, never planning to fulfill the promise.

He left her with an estate full of dead men, the looming prospect of life painted as a traitor, and the exhilarating knowledge that she'd taken back what was rightfully hers.

When she climbed back into bed in the early hours of the morning, her husband pulled her frozen limbs against his heated ones, letting her cold heart meld with his warm soul. She changed with each passing moment, and she feared more than anything leaving him behind.

Present

When Amalie woke that morning three years ago, the bodies of the slain royal guards were gone, but rumors remained. That was the day Tyson began seeing her for something other than the sweet noble lady he'd met at court. The one who'd spent her entire life believing she'd marry his brother, the king.

But still, he hadn't seen their end coming as she had. Tyson was always too good for his circumstances.

Now, she dug her heels into the flanks of her horse and wound through the village streets with Tuck close behind her. Feeling for her bow tied to the saddle behind her, she clenched her jaw. Her fault. If John hurt Tyson, she'd never forgive herself. Somehow, keeping her secret wasn't as important anymore. Protecting herself wasn't worth what could happen to Tyson out there among her men.

She snapped her reins, picking up speed as the horse's hooves pounded along the path leading from the village into the woods. Wild trees gave way to well-used and familiar paths that marked the way to the forest dwelling created by a few of her wanted men who could no longer show their faces in public.

She stopped at the twisted tree she knew so well. "I hope we aren't too late."

Tuck nodded grimly. They'd both known the type of men they consorted with. Even John, someone Amalie had known as a shy little boy, never tried to hide the danger inside him. She loved them all despite their darkness and sometimes because of it.

But she'd never expected that darkness to affect Tyson as well.

Rustling sounded from the trees behind her and she froze. As much as she wanted to save Tyson, she also didn't want outsiders stumbling upon the forest dwelling. Those who wouldn't understand her need to protect the rough men who lived there.

The enclave wasn't too far off the road. To any passing traveler, it only looked like a small grouping of simple folk... as long as they didn't linger long.

But someone was following her. She stepped off the path and her boots sank into the soft, leaf-covered floor. Tendrils of white moss hung from the branches above like a veil.

A stick snapped, and she gestured to Tuck as she raised her bow. Her friend had already drawn his sword and lunged into a bush to his left.

A grunt exited the twisted thicket before Tuck pulled Edmund free. Amalie breathed out heavily and lowered her weapon. "What are you doing hiding in the woods, Edmund?"

He pushed Tuck off him and rested a hand on the knife sticking from his belt, a move Amalie didn't miss.

Edmund's face darkened, a look she'd rarely seen on him. "I was looking for Tyson." He brushed his hand down his pants to rid them of the leaves clinging to the fabric.

"I figured." Amalie matched his scowl. "But that doesn't explain why you were in a bush."

"I saw them take him." He glanced to Tuck. "You told me to leave, but there's something you don't know about me. I never abandon my friends. I've been looking out for Tyson since before La Dame tried to destroy Bela. I'm sorry, but your word that no harm would come to him wasn't enough for me."

Amalie met his eyes. "What did you see? When they..." She swallowed. "Took him."

"A group of men I assume were working for you jumped him in an alley. I was watching at a distance but by the time I'd sprinted across the market square, they were gone. I tracked them to the woods, but heard someone coming and didn't have time to think. I jumped for the nearest cover."

It made sense. Tuck didn't know Edmund, but Amalie did. She knew Edmund would never allow Ty to be put in danger unless he was by his side.

Tyson wasn't any different. He'd give his life for Edmund. When they were wed, Tyson's desire to go home was one of the things tearing them apart. He felt he'd abandoned his family and was torn between staying with her and returning to Bela. She'd refused to move to Bela when she was needed in Gaule, but eventually she'd pushed him to go home.

Finally, she broke eye contact. "There are dwellings up ahead."

Edmund narrowed his eyes. "I know who you are, Amalie Leroy. And I don't trust you. If something happens to Tyson, nowhere will be safe for the Hood." He started walking. "I felt like you should know."

What she didn't say was if something happened to Tyson, there wasn't anywhere she'd hide. She'd let them have her.

"Edmund," she called. "I appreciate the threat and all, but I feel like I need to tell you something as well."

He froze, but kept his back to her. "What?"

"You're going the wrong way."

He turned and brushed past her without another word.

For so long, the Hood had been a mask she wore to protect her from herself. Amalie Leroy had lost everything. The Hood gave her a purpose. But what if that mask took from her as well? What if Tyson wasn't lost because of her family name, but her secret one?

Then who would she be?

How could she hide her brokenness when each face she wore bore the same cracks?

Chapter
Fourteen

Tyson struggled to retreat from the quiet of his own mind. Fog invaded the space between sleeping and waking. A dim light came into focus as he opened his eyes. A candle sat on a table beside where he lay on the floor of a one-room hovel.

His eyes searched the darkened surroundings. When had night come? A thin pallet lay only feet from him, so why was he on the packed dirt floor?

His head throbbed, a reminder of what happened. Someone abducted him. Was this how Simon disappeared too?

His eyes flew to the door as voices entered on the chilly breeze. The Hood could stand just on the other side of that door.

Tuck's words came back to him. He truly believed the Hood was a force for good. But no one good abducted a prince and held him prisoner.

A hand pushed the door flap open, revealing a man Tyson had seen twice before. Tyson's eyes widened, and he shook his head. John Little was supposed to be dead, shot by an arrow and buried in an unmarked grave outside the Gaulean palace walls.

The beard still coated his cheeks, but Tyson got the distinct impression it didn't belong there, as if the man was trying to hide.

He probably was. As soon as they'd realized his body was missing, his mother would have issued a warrant for the man's arrest.

A grim smile settled on John's face. "Hello, Prince Tyson."

Tyson ground his teeth together. "What does the Hood want with me?"

John stopped in front of him and crouched down. Tyson wasn't restrained. He could have attacked the Hood's man right there, but how many more were outside that door? He felt for his sword, knowing it was gone before brushing his hand over the empty scabbard. He could use his magic, but how many people would he have to kill?

John studied him for a moment. "The Hood does not know you're here, but she will understand."

Tyson's blood froze. She? After all his searching, this was his first clue. But to follow the lead, he'd have to get free.

"Listen to me, Prince, and listen closely. I don't want to hurt you. Believe it or not, the Hood doesn't appreciate violence. But I care more for protecting her than making her proud, so I will do what I must."

Tyson swallowed. "What do you want from me?"

John straightened. "The most valuable thing you own. Information." He reached down and hauled Tyson to his feet before pushing him out the door.

Tyson stumbled before righting himself and taking in his surroundings. Tall, thin trees stood in a circle around a clearing. At his back, a row of small ramshackle forest dwellings sat, looking as if mud and rusted nails held them together. Was this how people outside the villages lived?

Faces swam before him, each one rougher than the next. Hard eyes glared at him. These were the kind of people the Hood associated with? And yet, Tuck was convinced of the nobility of her fight.

There was nothing noble about these men. Only one woman stood among them, her skirt soiled with dirt. Thick black curls fell about her shoulders, and a grim smile slid across her lips. Tyson looked away.

How did he get here? A prisoner in the woods of a kingdom he both hated and loved. A prince tasked with a mission doomed to fail.

John gripped the back of his neck and urged him forward. "Welcome to our home, Prince." He gestured to the group before him. "Meet the Merry Men of the forest."

The Merry Men. He'd heard that term before.

John continued. "The king's guard raided a village four days ago. There were rumors of Hood impersonators tearing up the countryside." He bent and jerked Tyson's head back so their gazes locked. "Tell us everything you know."

Everything he knew? Tyson had never been invited to take part in any of his mother's schemes, but he had a hard time believing she'd ordered the raid of one of her own villages.

"I know nothing."

John released his head, straightened, and circled Tyson. His foot collided with Tyson's back, sending him sprawling into the dirt. He spit dirt and rocks from his mouth with a groan. A tingling began in his fingertips as his magic begged for an escape. He could end this right now, but what good would that do?

If he escaped now without resolution, they'd only come for him again. And they were his only connection to the Hood. If he wanted to succeed in his mission, he had to hold his power back. At least for now.

Getting his arms under him, he pushed himself onto his knees.

John paced in front of him. "I know of the power you possess, Tyson Durand. And I do not fear it. You need us as much as we need you."

"You have some way of showing it." Tyson wiped the dirt from his face.

John stopped moving. "When are they coming?"

"Who?"

"The guard!" His scream echoed through the woods. "When will they be upon us? How much time do we have to evacuate our people from the village?"

Tyson pulled back in surprise. How many of them were there? If he was being honest, he hoped the guard wouldn't come at all. His mother sent him on this mission for a reason. She'd betrayed Amalie once when she took control of the Leroy estate—even if she never believed Amalie would return to Gaule. She wouldn't send in the guard to terrorize a village on the Leroy lands. But as long as Simon was missing, the queen would be unpredictable.

Yet, there was a reason they'd called Tyson from Bela. He was the one person his mother thought could accomplish anything under the watchful eye of Amalie.

She'd underestimated the girl's hatred of the prince.

Tyson didn't tell them that. He didn't say there was nothing to fear yet. Instead, he climbed to his feet.

A few of the people watching drew their weapons.

Tyson ignored them. He saw his chance and had no choice but to take it. "The guard moves swiftly over the land, giving my mother a long reach. It's almost too late. You'll never get your people out in time."

"How long?" John growled.

"Even if I knew the answer, I wouldn't tell you."

A roar ripped from John and he slammed his fist into Tyson's stomach. Tyson doubled over, trying to catch his breath. A force drove him to his knees, and his magic swirled within. It wanted to fight, was meant to fight.

A kick knocked him onto his side. The last thing he saw was a boot flying toward his head as a piercing scream ripped through the air.

"Noooooo!"

Amalie?

But he was already gone, lost in a darkness where the sun never rose.

Chapter Fifteen

"John!" Amalie ran into the clearing. She was too late.

John froze with his knife hovering over Tyson's still form. "You shouldn't be here, Amalie."

"And neither should you." She pushed through her men who were looking anywhere but at her. She'd had no delusions about those she allied herself with, but seeing them hover over an unconscious Tyson, made her rethink every choice she'd made since becoming the Hood.

She dropped to her knees at Tyson's side and felt his neck for the telltale thumping that would allow her to breathe again.

Tuck and Edmund moved to each side of her, keeping John at a distance. She dropped her bow on the ground and pushed the hair out of Tyson's face.

He never changed. When the world turned around them, everything becoming unrecognizable, his face remained the same.

Tears pushed at her eyelids, but she refused to let her men see how much Tyson meant to her. He was supposed to be the past, a pretty fantasy crafted by a girl who'd been raised to be a noble lady. The Hood was emotionless, strong.

When two worlds collided, she no longer wanted to be strong.

Edmund, sword drawn, pointed it at Alan, Gilbert, and Regina who watched them with cautious eyes. They wouldn't come near or threaten them, not while she was there. But Edmund didn't know that. He didn't know that she'd suffered much alongside these people. That they'd become her family when she'd had none. That they'd healed her when she was broken.

Tuck put a hand on Edmund's arm. "It's okay. They aren't a threat."

Edmund shifted his glare to Tuck. "We found them beating Tyson into unconsciousness and you tell me they aren't a threat? I could kill them for what they did, and it would be well deserved."

Amalie had once wished someone was as loyal to her as Edmund, Tyson, and Alex had always been to each other. She'd longed for that kind of bond.

Now that she had it, it threatened to drown every other part of her life. She flattened her palm against Tyson's chest one final time before wrapping her fingers around her bow and standing.

She hated what they'd done to Tyson, but it had a purpose. "What did he tell you?"

Edmund turned to her. "That's what you care about? They abducted him and beat him, yet this is what you do now? Will we find Simon beaten in some cell?"

Amalie ignored him, focusing on John.

John glanced once more at Tyson before facing her. "Nothing. The man is as useless as he always was."

She shook her head. John hadn't known Tyson well. After Ty left, she'd sent John with a letter she hoped would bring

Tyson back to her. In it, she wrote the words that should have shaped their future, but that letter was written by a scared girl facing her own mortality. Tyson never returned, and all John brought her were regrets from the man she'd thought had loved her.

She shook the thought from her mind. That was a long time ago. As long as Anders never found what she protected on the Caron lands, she may never have to introduce Tyson to that side of her life.

The Tyson she knew never would have given information freely. He'd been imprisoned by La Dame herself and escaped. Her brow furrowed. "Why didn't he use his magic? He could have stopped this."

"You don't know him at all." Edmund slid his sword into its sheathe. "Tyson never uses his magic for himself. Not since La Dame. The only time I've seen him use it was in Madra because he knew it was the only way to save Estevan... for me."

He bent to slide his arms under Tyson's still form and hoisted him into his arms. "You can try to stop me, but I'm taking Tyson. Maiya can heal him. By morning, we won't be your problem anymore."

"What do you mean?"

"Anders will return soon to continue seeking the Hood. Tyson and I will leave the mission to him and return to Bela, the kingdom we never should have left. You broke him once, Amalie, and it seems you never stop trying to hurt him. You and your people call your mission noble, but you're nothing more than thieves and thugs."

His words slammed into Amalie like a bludgeon to the chest. She sucked in a breath, holding in the tears trying to spill down her cheeks.

As Edmund disappeared into the trees, Tuck stepped up beside her. "Go," she pleaded. "Help him. Please. I... I can't."

Tuck only nodded and took off after Edmund.

Her chest heaved with the effort of containing the emotions ravaging her mind. A thick drop of water struck her cheek. For a moment, she thought it was a tear, but then another came and another as the torrent of rain broke free of the thick clouds overhead.

People scrambled into their homes, but Amalie remained, staring up into the dark void of the night.

All of her reasons for choosing this life suddenly seemed as murky as the dark clouds above. She kept the village fed through thievery and deception. Did that make her the criminal everyone said she was?

One thing was clear. If Tyson knew the mask she wore—or hood in her case—he'd never see her the same way. Even through the pain swirling in the air every time they saw each other, she hadn't missed the longing in his eyes. She wasn't delusional enough to think it was for her, only for what they had. But he'd forsaken her when he refused to return with John two years ago.

Would she go back to what they were when they were younger?

She pushed wet strands of hair back from her face. No. That answer came unbidden, but it was the truth. She was more herself traipsing through the woods and firing arrows at her targets than she'd ever been in pretty dresses attending balls.

Yet, she wasn't a warrior. She'd gone to war, fighting both her father's force and La Dame's. There was an emptiness in battle, a lingering void she felt even now.

She didn't want to take lives or abduct good people. Simon was comfortable in a seldom-used wing of the Leroy estate, but he wasn't free.

She rubbed a hand against her stomach, longing for a life she'd once felt with every inch of her being.

A presence hovered behind her. She sighed, her feelings toward her best friend on the edge of hatred. "Go inside, John. You'll catch a chill."

He tried to slip his hand into hers, but she pulled away. "Ames," he sighed. "You know it had to be done. He deserved everything he received after abandoning you."

Over the years, John had never missed an opportunity to disparage Tyson. Tuck once claimed it was because John felt more than friendship for Amalie. But Amalie could never see him or any man in that way. Not again. She'd given all her love to those who could not give it back. One who abandoned her. And another she'd abandoned.

She turned to him so fast, she collided with his chest and stumbled back. "Be glad he survived because I would never forgive you."

"He isn't one of us, Amalie. Don't forget that. Tyson Durand is a prince, loyal to the queen who has nothing but disdain for the likes of us. You'd do well to get your priorities straight."

She scowled, barely feeling the rain that continued to fall, creating a curtain between them. "And you'd do well to remember who I am."

He laughed. "The Hood? I made you."

"I don't even know who you are anymore." She turned on her heel to storm away but he gripped her arm, holding her back.

"I'm the same man I've always been."

She closed her eyes, images of the dead guards flashing in her mind. He'd shown her who he truly was the night she set him free. Not the boy she'd known as a child or a man who wanted to keep the people of the village fed.

She'd failed to believe his true face then because he'd

offered her a life beyond the high walls of the estate. He was right. He'd turned her into the vigilante she'd become.

She ripped her arm free. "It's time I become who I want to be."

He didn't follow her as she trudged to where her horse was still tied. As she freed the reins, climbed on, and left the forest behind, she realized what she should have known all along. The Hood was an excuse, a way to fight back in the shadows when she should have braved the light of day.

Chapter

Sixteen

Two years ago

Tyson always slept so peacefully. It was one of the things Amalie envied about him. But then when morning came, the restlessness in his eyes never left.

He didn't want to be there. They'd been at her estate for months now, involved in running the Leroy lands. Each day, Tyson ventured into the village and each day, he grew more distant.

At night, he never woke. Not when Amalie slipped from the bed to join John in the forest for her lessons with the bow. Not now when she returned, weary and satisfied.

If she were honest, her time training with John was the only hours of the day or night she enjoyed.

The queen hadn't sent more guards to the estate when hers went missing. Tyson said she accepted that they were staying. He made excuses for his mother, saying she hadn't wanted the estate to fall into the hands of people who'd been loyal to her father. The lands were too valuable.

No one thought they'd return, and she knew Tyson questioned that decision every day.

But not her. She knew in her heart it had been right. The people living on her family's lands suffered, and she wanted to help them.

Tyson stormed into the room where she'd sat drinking her morning tea. She hoped he couldn't see the weariness on her face.

He dropped into a chair. "Did you hear? Someone attacked a trade caravan on our roads last night."

"Really?" She sipped her tea, trying to ignore the guilt building within her. Tyson was too honest for his own good. He'd never understand what she'd started, or that she spent her nights with an old friend instead of her husband.

"We have to do something about this. We have enough trouble getting food and goods to the village without traders avoiding our roads."

Amalie set her cup down. "Those traders rarely stop in the village to unload their wares. They use our roads to get to the Caron lands. Another gift from your mother, I assume." She couldn't hide the scowl on her face.

Tyson leaned forward, resting his elbows on his knees. "My mother has nothing to do with that."

She raised an eyebrow. "My people are tainted, Ty. They fought for a traitor. It doesn't matter to anyone else that my father forced them into it."

Tyson sighed. It was a conversation they'd had with more frequency of late. He refused to see her side of things. But what had she expected? She knew his true loyalty was never hers. He'd pledged himself to his mother, his brother, and his sister, Etta, before his wife. They took precedence in his mind. Duty trumped love, though he loved them all too.

She thought she'd accepted it. That she could live with never being first in his heart.

But with each passing day, it only hurt more, breaking off pieces of her own heart. Soon, she feared there would be nothing left.

"I don't want to argue, Ty." She stood and moved to sit on the arm of his chair, wrapping her arms around him.

"You know how much I love you, right?" He peered up at her, every ounce of sincerity he possessed shining in his eyes.

She nodded, because it was the truth. She did know how much he loved her. Tyson had never been hard to read. His openness was one of the reasons she'd been drawn to him over his more serious brother. He had an innate goodness she feared was slipping away.

Because as much as he loved her, it wasn't enough. She needed more.

And so did he.

Present

By the time Amalie returned to the estate, the silence of the night echoed through the empty halls. She roused a stable boy who'd been dozing on a hay bale and left her horse's care to him. As she walked her tired limbs up the front steps, she unclasped her sopping cloak. A shiver raced through her, the cold finally settling in to her bones.

But she couldn't return to her rooms. Not yet. She had to see him. To remember the parts of herself she'd tried so hard to forget and confront the parts she'd wanted to hide.

Her pants stuck to her legs as she strolled through the familiar and somehow haunting halls. So much had happened there. Her boots left wet prints behind her, a reminder that she'd been there.

As she got to Tyson's room, Edmund stepped into the hall and closed the door behind him. He'd changed into dry clothing, and his wet hair was pulled back into a tail.

He didn't scowl when he saw her. That was something. Instead, weariness coated his features. "I'm not going to let you in there."

She could have retorted with something about it being her house, but that didn't seem to matter anymore, so she accepted Edmund's words. "How is he?"

"Maiya healed the bruises."

"Did he... did you get to talk to him?" She bit her lip and pulled her arms across her shaking body.

He sighed. "Ty... dammit! He should have used his magic." He rubbed the back of his neck in agitation. "He gave me some noble bullshit about not using it against non-magic folk, but his life was in danger."

"They wouldn't have killed him."

"You don't know that." Edmund paced across the hall before turning. "You can't control your people."

She wondered if she'd ever had control over them. Their loyalty to her hadn't changed who they were. She thought back on the attacks that had gone too far. The traders and waggoneers who'd been hurt. She'd allowed men with less noble goals into her circle because John told her they'd needed them. She cared about her friend, believing he was truly as good as he'd claimed.

She glanced at the door to Tyson's room. But who was as good as the man on the other side? Certainly not her.

A weight pressed down on her shoulder and it took her a moment to realize it was Edmund's hand.

His expression softened. "Come on, Ames." His use of her

nickname calmed her troubled mind as she remembered she was safe with Edmund. He'd only ever tried to help her.

He slid his palm down her arm and took her hand. "I need a drink."

She only nodded and allowed him to pull her down the hall. She paid no attention to their location in the house or the time it took them to reach another closed door with two guards standing on each side of it.

Her eyes finally focused, and a small gasp escaped her. "You knew."

He looked sideways at her. "Of course I knew. I'm me."

She would have laughed in any other circumstances. Sometimes she forgot this was a man who ran a network of spies in Madra before the rebellion, or the man who stood by Persinette Basile's side as she fought for Bela. He'd been the best swordsman in Gaule, but he'd also always just been Edmund, fighting for his friends and keeping secrets every step of the way.

He still hadn't told Tyson her identity as the Hood, and she didn't know why.

She nodded to the guards in greeting and knocked. A voice she knew well told her to enter.

Simon sat in the same chair she'd found him in during her last visit. Still calm. Still a prisoner. He showed no surprise at Edmund's presence. "Edmund," he smiled. "It's been a long time."

Edmund rushed forward to grip his hand. "Simon, it's damn good to see you. Everyone is worried."

Simon released him and leaned back. "I decided a visit to Amalie was in order."

"Bullshit." Edmund walked to the table along the back wall to pour three glasses of wine.

Amalie, still in her wet clothes, crossed the room to the fireplace where flames danced, casting their glow about the room.

Edmund appeared at her side and handed her a glass.

She sipped the burgundy wine, letting the warmth flood her limbs. Once her teeth stopped chattering, she spoke. "Simon is a prisoner; how did you know he'd have wine?"

One corner of Edmund's mouth curved up. "You think you've changed, Amalie, but I have watched Tyson mourn for the last two years as if you'd died. You try to hide it, but you do the same." He took a long drink. "No, Ames. You haven't changed. You're still the girl in a situation she can't control who is irreparably in love with a man she doesn't think she can have."

"That doesn't answer my question." Her voice shook.

"The girl I knew wouldn't hurt Simon, and she definitely wouldn't coop him up without wine."

Amalie couldn't help the laugh that rolled through her. "You say that as if wine is essential to life."

"Isn't it?"

She shook her head. "Still the same old drunkard, I see."

His expression darkened for a moment and when he smoothed his features, she wondered if she'd imagined it.

Simon, who'd been watching them, cleared his throat. "Edmund, if you're here, I can only assume Tyson has come as well."

Edmund threw himself down into a high-backed chair. The firelight reflected off his blue eyes, making them dance. "He's asleep at the moment."

Simon shifted his gaze from Edmund to Amalie and back again. "He's either avoiding Miss Leroy here or something has happened that you aren't telling me."

Amalie stepped closer to the fire, trying to let the crackling of the wood drown out the pounding of her heart. There was a time when Simon's council had been that of a father's. She once cared for him like family. But she had to remember he was the queen's most trusted guard, the man Catrine loved. Which meant she could no longer put her trust in him.

The disappearance of the royal guards who'd controlled her estate was never investigated. The queen let it rest, but if the truth were ever revealed... if Simon learned Amalie had a hand in murdering his comrades, the kindness in his eyes would disappear. And that... she couldn't take.

She had a talent for stripping the best qualities from a person. One only need to look at Tyson to see what she could do.

Edmund leaned forward. "He's okay, Si."

Simon seemed to relax. "Does he know?"

Edmund shook his head.

She didn't have to ask what Simon meant. There were so many secrets she'd kept from Ty. Her identity as the Hood. The fact that John, the man who'd beaten him, was one of her closest friends.

The whereabouts of the one person Ty should want to see. Yet he hadn't asked, and she hadn't offered the information freely. Maybe he didn't care after all.

Then there was Simon's presence in the estate.

That was the big one. The Tyson she knew could forgive her for anything else, but holding Simon prisoner was a different matter altogether.

Even if she'd kept him in comfort.

She couldn't stand to stare at Simon anymore. He represented every awful thing she'd done. Without a word to either man, she set her glass down on the table and turned on her heel to march toward the door.

Once out in the hall, she glanced sideways at two of the guards. Part of her wanted to tell them they could abandon their posts. Maybe it was better if she allowed Simon to leave.

Something stopped her. She opened her mouth and the

words that came out sounded foreign to her ears. "Watch Edmund carefully. He has magic, just as Simon does. Don't let him cause any problems."

The guard closest ducked his head. "Yes, lady Leroy."

As she walked away, his words blazed in her mind. *Lady Leroy.* She wasn't one of them. Her family betrayed the realm again and again. Was she just following in her father's shadow?

A chill raced down her spine and this time, it had nothing to do with the cold.

Chapter Seventeen

Two Years Ago

"Amalie." Tyson's voice broke as pain unlike anything he felt before seared through him.

His flesh had burned in a village fire. He'd faced La Dame and almost lost the people closest to him.

But it was the girl before him who finally broke his will.

Magic seeped from his fingertips, little drops of water breaking free as if it wept the tears Tyson held back.

Amalie shook her head, her long chestnut hair blowing into her face as the wind swept through the courtyard. He wanted to reach out and brush it back, to feel her skin one more time and pretend nothing had changed between them.

When everything had changed. He'd felt it for months. The distance. Amalie thought he didn't notice her slipping from the estate late at night. He never followed her because he feared what he'd find.

Another man. Some dark secret she wouldn't even tell her

best friend. That's what they'd been once. Friends. Confidants. He couldn't help but wonder if they'd stayed that way, maybe he wouldn't have to lose her. He would have been content riding by her side his entire life even if it meant he never knew her touch in the dark of the night.

They'd fought the night before when he demanded to know what was going on. He'd felt the finality of her words.

'Maybe I wasn't destined for marriage,' she'd said. 'I want to have a greater purpose'.

He'd tried many times to convince her to leave the estate behind. To travel to Bela where they could have served Etta and lived for more than overseeing staff and training for battles that never came.

"I need you to leave, Ty." She held her arms across her chest as if protecting it from the pain in his eyes.

"I don't have to obey this." He held up the paper they'd received a week before. A summons to the palace of Gaule. To his mother. They'd spoken of it every day since, but Amalie still didn't see. He loved his mother, but he'd have given her up. Yet she never believed him. She claimed he'd always choose his family.

He'd have given everything up.

So, he told her.

Her hard eyes met his. "That's the problem, Ty. We shouldn't have to give up our lives for each other. I don't want to be a princess. I don't want to be beholden to the crown of Gaule or Bela."

He didn't understand. She'd always known who he was. "I'm not beholden to anyone but you."

"Yes, you are." She reached out but then pulled her hand back. "The Tyson Durand I fell in love with would do anything for his family. I may not love your mother anymore, but you need to go to her if she needs you."

"I don't."

She took his hand. "I've seen you change over the last year as you've lived in this house. As you've experienced the damage done by my father. He's dead, but his soul remains. It taints everything here. I don't want that for you."

"I want you." Tears gathered in his eyes.

She pulled her hand from his and drove the final dagger into his heart. "But I don't want you. Not anymore."

The pain in his gaze hardened, turning into unbridled anger. One of the stable lads appeared with a horse and Tyson turned toward the beast.

He climbed on and looked down at Amalie once more. "I will always love you, Amalie Leroy, but it seems like that isn't enough."

He rode through the gates without another thought and dug his heels in to cantor down the road. Amalie had taken everything from him, and the emptiness threatened to consume him.

The magic he'd held back in the year since fighting La Dame poured from him, pulling the rain from the clouds above. He thought he'd lost his desire for battle since the war, but now all he wanted was to join in a fight. He didn't answer the summons from his mother.

Instead, he turned toward the roads leading into Bela. His mother had always told him home was where his heart resided. But what happened when that heart cracked and its once steady rhythm faded into nothing?

Present

Amalie's feet took her to Tyson's door once more. But this time, she didn't stop herself from entering. Thunder ripped through the sky outside his window, and a flash of light lit the room. The maids had allowed his fire to dwindle, and she suddenly wished she'd gone for dry clothes before coming here.

But she couldn't leave. Tyson lay on the bed with his legs tangled up in the blankets. His bare chest rose and fell steadily. After his healing, she doubted he'd wake anytime soon.

All her reasons for making him leave two years ago no longer made any sense.

I don't want you. Not anymore.

It was the greatest lie she'd ever told. The truth was, she'd been on the edge of what she thought was the biggest purpose in her life. He'd have known better. He wouldn't have understood.

And she didn't want to be stopped.

The Hood needed to exist. After Tyson left, the only time she felt alive was when she ran through the woods with her bow in her hand.

She pulled a chair to the side of the bed and sat, never once taking her eyes from Tyson's innocent face. That was the thing about him. No matter his age, no matter his fight he never lost the pure innocence.

A tear slid down her cheek as she thought of the weeks following his departure. She'd thrown herself into training with John, running her body into exhaustion just to keep her mind occupied.

She'd treated Ty so poorly the last time she'd seen him. What he hadn't known was how each night he'd spent under her roof had broken her.

"I'm so sorry, Ty," she whispered. "This is all my fault."

She leaned her forehead on the bed as more thunder rumbled through the room.

"Not your fault."

At first, she thought she'd imagined the voice because it was so faint, but then a hand brushed over the back of her head. She choked back a sob and lifted her head.

Tyson's eyes slid open, and she recognized the exhaustion in their depths.

She pulled away from his hand.

His gaze held hers. "Why would you say this is your fault? I was abducted by some men in the forest. I'm assuming Edmund found me if I'm here."

She closed her eyes, and another tear squeezed between the lids. "The man who took you..."

"I know," he said quickly. "He was sentenced to death. He shouldn't be alive. I know he was a friend of yours and that you were at the palace to save him. Looks like the Hood did your job."

He watched her carefully, but she didn't react. "I guess the Hood did one thing good." She cringed as soon as the words left her mouth. John had just beaten Tyson unconscious. His survival wasn't something Ty would want to celebrate. She shifted her gaze away from him.

Tyson grabbed her hand. "Hey, it's okay. He was important to you. Regardless of his actions, that feeling doesn't go away."

She wiped away the tears threatening to spill forth. "Why are you being so kind to me? After everything I did... you should hate me."

He released her hand to scratch his face. "I don't know, Ames. For so long, I thought I did, but being here with you feels..." He shook his head. "I can't hate you."

Unable to believe his kindness after everything that had passed between them, she pulled her hand back and stood. "I must find some dry clothes and my bed." She walked swiftly to the door and stopped with her hand on the latch. Without turning back, she sucked in a shuddering breath. "I'm glad you're okay. Goodnight, your Highness."

When she returned to her room, she ripped off her clothing, wanting to rid herself of any memory of that night. Flashes of an unconscious Tyson took hold of her mind. She closed her eyes and rested her hand on the icy skin of her chest, letting her own heartbeat calm her. He was okay.

Tyson was always okay. No matter what he did, he found a way out of it. Join the battle with La Dame—not even a scratch. Fight a usurper across the sea in Madra—no problem for the prince of two kingdoms. Father a child and refuse to return—it didn't even weigh on his mind.

He acted like their life together had never happened. Like she hadn't sent John to Bela with a letter begging Tyson to return, revealing the baby that grew inside her.

By the time she'd realized she was pregnant, he was gone, and the Hood had already become a renowned figure. She hadn't stopped her mission, scaling walls and running through the woods. Fighting men twice her size at night and then pretending she was nothing more than Lady Leroy during the day.

But then the pains came along with a torrent of blood. It had been too early, and the healer feared for both Amalie and the baby's lives. The baby was born, and she'd said her goodbyes while waiting for Tyson to come.

When John returned, he only brought Tyson's refusal and Maiya, the young magic woman. Amalie closed her eyes, remembering the feel of Maiya's healing magic warming her skin.

It had changed nothing regarding the child. Whether Amalie lived or died, she couldn't involve someone so helpless in the life of an outlaw. Her enemies would come. At the very least, the queen would if she knew of the birth of her grandchild. No, Amalie couldn't have anything more tying her to the regent she betrayed with every draw of her bowstring.

The Leroys were traitors. Amalie only carried on the family business. The goodness of her mission wouldn't matter to Catrine. Or Tyson.

Her eyes snapped open. What would he say if he knew of her occupation?

She took the silk nightgown from a hook near the washroom and slipped it on over her head before crawling into her bed and wrapping her shivering frame in soft furs. Exhaustion won out over conscious thought and she drifted into slumber.

Chapter Eighteen

Throughout the next day, Amalie attended to matters of the estate. She inspected a crumbling part of the walls, approved the next week's meager menu with the cooks, and met with townsfolk who pleaded for her intercession in disputes of land ownership.

What she did not do was visit Tyson's room. He should be mostly recovered by now with only a little weakness lingering.

Edmund was a constant presence in the halls, walking from Tyson's room to Simon's and back again. He held so many secrets inside him, and she still didn't understand why he kept hers from Tyson. Those two were as close as brothers.

He walked up beside her as she entered the great hall for supper. When she didn't have guests, she was the only person to occupy the long table. She'd grown used to eating alone. Solitude suited her, but she also missed a time when laughter echoed throughout the room.

"How has your day progressed, Duchess?" Edmund smirked

as though he knew how his use of the formal title she no longer held vexed her.

"Busy."

He nodded, accepting her terse tone. "Tyson has healed well."

"I didn't ask."

"But you wanted to." He seated himself at the table without waiting for her and glanced up.

She sank into a chair, smoothing the skirt of her dress over her legs. "Do you enjoy irritating me?"

"Very much so." He flashed her a smile and reached for the pitcher of wine to fill both their cups. "In truth, Ames, Ty has been a pain in the... uh rear today."

She sipped her wine, trying to hide her curiosity.

Edmund continued. "He's restless."

She snorted and slapped a hand over her mouth.

Edmund's grin widened. "Very lady-like, Ames."

Pulling her hand away, she took another sip. "I'm sorry. It's just that some things never change. Tyson has always had a restless soul."

Edmund smiled at the servant who set a plate of salted fish and roast potatoes in front of him. He leaned toward Amalie as if sharing some great secret. "It's the energy. He has too much of it. He always has to have some purpose, and sitting still just does not suit him. It's why he jumped at the chance to help Helena reclaim the Madran throne. Not only to save his sister, Camille, but also to have a mission."

Amalie had always seen that in Ty, but in recent years, she'd found the same to be true of herself. "I know the feeling."

"I imagine you do."

"Can I ask you something, Edmund?"

He stuffed a forkful of potato into his mouth and nodded.

"Why haven't you told him?" She busied herself with her own supper while waiting for his answer.

He sighed and set his fork on the table. "Because the woman he loves is running around Gaule risking her life with each mission she takes on. Because, I suspect your need to help the people drove you to send Tyson back to Bela with a broken heart." He met her gaze. "Because, though I worry about you and the company you keep, I believe in what you're doing." He lifted his eyes to the ceiling as if he couldn't believe his own words. "What is it with the women in my life and their penchant for trouble?"

She laughed at that. Edmund was loyal to Persinette Basile, queen of Bela, who served her people in any way she could—just as Amalie wished to. Amalie had no love for royals or nobles, but Etta was different. And Alex, the king of Bela, many in Gaule held no love for him, but he'd always tried to do the right thing.

Edmund's next words pulled her from her own thoughts. "For the record, Ames, Ty would too. If you let him."

"He would what?"

"Believe in you."

The door to the hall burst open and Will entered, his large stature making the room seem smaller. Upon seeing the seriousness of his expression, Amalie rose from her chair. "What is it?"

"Captain Anders has been spotted in the village."

The mercenary's words took a moment to register. She didn't know where Anders had gone when he disappeared, but she'd known he'd return. With Ty here, Anders wasn't the only one searching for the Hood on her lands, but she'd never worried Tyson posed the same threat.

"I'm coming." She skirted the edge of the table. Edmund rose to follow her, and she shook her head. "Stay here."

"He's my father, Amalie. Let me help."

She turned back to face him. "He may be your father, but he has been tasked with arresting me just as you and Tyson have. I don't want your help. This is a problem for the Hood, and I'm sorry Edmund, but I have my own people to stand at my side. Men I trust. You and Tyson will stay within these walls."

She marched from the room with Will following. "Where is Anders now?"

"At the tavern, my lady."

Nodding, she turned the corner to enter her room. "You and Cameron will accompany me. We'll set up watch posts. I want eyes on the captain for the duration of his stay."

Will left to retrieve Cameron as Amalie changed into a pair of trousers and a tunic. She stepped into her boots, slung a quiver over her shoulder and left the room with her bow in one hand and hood in the other. She couldn't put the hood on until she was away from the estate walls.

In the courtyard, Will and Cameron waited. She spoke no words to them as she led them through the gates. They'd know what to do.

She'd spent years training and running missions with the same men. Each knew their roles. Each could anticipate the actions of the others.

She wasn't lying when she told Edmund she didn't trust him. Not in the way she trusted those who'd fought injustice by her side. The ones who risked everything for her.

The moon rose high above them, full save for a missing sliver. No stars dotted the clear sky. The darkened streets held few dangers. Her band of men kept a tight rein on the village. A breeze whipped between the buildings, and it was only then she remembered she'd forgotten her cloak.

Clenching her teeth against the cold, she used the torches outside the tavern as a beacon. Raucous laughter sounded every time the heavy wooden doors opened and spilled men onto the street.

She gestured to Will to take up a position in the alley beside the tavern. Cameron left to enlist a few more of their men for the rotation the next day. Amalie glanced to each side before crossing the street and entering an alley. It was so familiar. This was where guards chased her and John up onto the roof before they had arrested him.

She pulled herself up the same way she had before and ran across the tiles with light steps until she could peer down at the tavern. She knelt down and set her bow beside her, preparing for a long night of watch.

TYSON PACED the length of the room before turning and walking back again. The door opened, and he turned as Edmund walked in.

He opened his mouth to speak, but Edmund put up a hand. "Ty, I have kept something from you and you're going to be angry with me, but there's time enough for that later."

"What are you talking about?" Tyson lifted a brow.

Edmund shook his head. "You aren't going to believe me unless you see it for yourself." He paused for a long moment. "The Hood is in the village right now."

Tyson stilled. "What? How could you possibly know that?"

"There's no time to explain. My father has returned, and I think the Hood is in danger. The information said he was alone, but he never travels alone. Our archer friend is walking into a trap. I'm sure of it."

Tyson crossed the room and slapped the side of Edmund's head. "Have you gone mad, man? We're here to arrest the criminal. If Anders succeeds, we'll be able to find Simon."

"Ty, do you trust me?"

"Of course I do."

"Then we have to go."

Tyson watched him for a moment longer. Edmund was the most honorable man he knew. He always did the right thing. If he truly thought the Hood needed their help, Tyson could set his doubts aside.

He reached for his sword belt and tied it around his waist before pulling on a cloak and grabbing his bow. Edmund already had his weapon ready, so they left without another word.

At the gates, the guard only nodded to them. They'd long since realized no one in the estate cared what happened to the prince. They were a land of people more loyal to their duchess than their queen.

Tyson should have been troubled by it, but he'd seen first-hand how Amalie gained the trust of even the toughest, crudest men.

"Edmund, I'm not going to ask where you get your information. Not yet. But I need all of it. Where was Anders seen?"

"The tavern."

Tyson nodded as his eyes adjusted to the darkness, lit only by the silver moon from up high. "Come on."

They neared the tavern. "You can guarantee the Hood is near?" A shiver raced down Tyson's spine. He'd heard many stories of the criminal he now knew was a woman. She fought for those who couldn't, but her aim was deadly accurate, and the wanted men who traveled with her were loyal.

Noise drifted from the tavern, and they ducked into a nearby alleyway. Tyson's feet collided with something on the ground. He bent to see what he'd kicked, and his breath lodged in his throat.

"Edmund," he hissed. "It's Will. One of the estate guards."

Edmund cursed and bent to feel for a pulse. "He's alive." He felt lower before pulling his hand back. Blood coated his skin.

Tyson rolled Will over to find a small knife wound in his stomach. Blood seeped out between the folds of skin.

"Dammit!" Edmund kicked the wall. "I knew this was a trap."

"Shit, Edmund." Tyson pressed a hand to Will's wound and looked up at his panicked friend. "I think the time has come to cease keeping secrets."

Edmund turned his back to Tyson and breathed out. When he spoke, his voice rumbled through the air. "Will is one of the Merry Men."

Tyson's eyes widened. "He's the Hood's man?"

Edmund finally turned to face him. "You need to go Ty. I'll help Will. The Hood needs you. Ander's guards knew he'd be watched. They counted on it. They'll find her."

"Why me?" Tyson swallowed. "Why is she our concern? Stop lying to me, Edmund."

"You don't need me to say it, Ty."

Tyson pulled his hand away from Will and jumped to his feet. He stumbled back. It couldn't be true. "Amalie," he whispered, knowing the truth in his gut. He should have known the moment he saw John alive.

He'd have to sort through it all later, because she needed him. He ran from the alley, scanning the rooftops as he did. She'd have to be around there somewhere. A troop of palace guards ran along the shadows on the other side of the street that led toward the woods. Their recognizable armor shone in the moonlight. Anders wouldn't be among them. Tyson was sure of it. But they'd find the Hood's trail.

He sprinted after them, veering off the stone streets of the village to head into the woods he'd never wanted to visit again.

"I'm coming, Ames."

Drawing his sword, he prepared to meet the first group of guards. He lifted his free hand, curling his fingers into a fist to draw moisture from the damp earth. His magic molded it, expanded it. He'd almost reached them when he opened his palm, sending a blast of water at the three guards. The force knocked them to the ground sputtering. Before they could pick themselves up, Tyson was there with his sword.

He told himself he was doing the right thing. These guards weren't his mother's normal men. No, they belonged to Anders, and the captain only accepted those into his service who took no issue with finding wanted men of Gaule by any means necessary. They terrorized villages, stole from the poor, and brutalized any who held information.

Tyson's sword cut a clean path through the men. They never stood a chance.

He didn't slow even as his legs grew heavy. Using that amount of magic weakened him after his recent injuries.

He curled his fingers tighter around the hilt of his sword and pushed through hanging branches, stumbling over a fallen tree.

He didn't slow until he caught sight of more guards surrounding a small figure in a hood. She shifted from foot to foot, never lowering her bow.

"Try to come closer." She turned to aim the arrow at a guard behind her. "I dare you."

The four guards advanced as one, and the Hood danced between them, dodging arcs of their swords. She released an arrow, striking one of the guards in the neck. She nocked a new one before he'd even collapsed.

The guard in front lunged toward her, and she bent backward. The sword skimmed the front of her tunic, missing her body entirely. When she straightened, she wasted no time in pulling another arrow free and ramming it under the guard's chin.

Two more.

Tyson reached her as she fought one guard. The second jumped for her, his sword almost reaching her back before Ty's blade blocked it.

Tyson kicked his foot out, catching the man in the stomach. He grunted, but didn't fall. All sound from the other fight ceased as Tyson continued to fight off the man in front of him. Their blades locked together.

"I know you, Prince," the guard growled. "Why do you protect this whore?"

Anger burned through Tyson, and his magic swirled in his fingertips. Water rose from the earth, and the guard's eyes widened seconds before a torrent of water flooded his throat. He coughed and sputtered, dropping his sword.

Tyson release the last of his magic, and the guard crumbled to the ground.

A voice sounded behind Tyson. "You drowned him."

Tyson's shoulders dropped as the energy drained from him. He turned toward the Hood, the shadows still hiding her face. But he knew her. He'd always known her.

He crossed the space between them in three strides and pushed back her hood.

Amalie's wide eyes greeted him, and relief flooded his mind. She was safe.

"Ty," she whispered. "I'm—"

He cut off her words by crushing his lips to hers. She stilled for only a moment before gripping his shoulders and spinning him so his back hit the nearest tree.

Adrenaline raced through him, and he remembered Amalie's every dip, every curve. The shape of her lips had once been burned into his mind. He'd tried so hard to forget, but he realized in that moment, there was no forgetting Amalie Leroy.

She gave him life.

He pressed his palms against the rough bark of the tree and rested his forehead against hers. "Why didn't you tell me?"

"Ty," she breathed. "Your mother sent you here to hunt me down."

He wished he could erase every bit of pain in her eyes. "You had to know I'd have protected you. Always."

A tear slid down her cheek, and he wiped it away before kissing her once again. This time, he took it slow, soaking in every emotion she brought out in him.

She put a hand to his chest and pushed him away with a shake of her head. "Don't you get it, Ty? I can protect myself now. I needed you once, and you didn't come." She brushed past him, but he grabbed her arm.

"Ames, you forced me to leave. I didn't have a choice."

She pulled her arm free. "And when I called for you? When I sent John with the letter? What then?"

"I don't know what you're talking about. Ames, you know me."

She stepped away. "I thought I did once. I won't make the same mistake again."

Her feet crashed through leaves and sticks as she widened the distance between them until Tyson couldn't see her anymore. He leaned back against the tree and rested a finger against his lips.

Chapter Nineteen

Two Years Ago

Death came calling as Amalie thrashed her head from side to side. Pain ripped through her, and she knew her end was near. At least the child was now free of its mother's ailing body. A healthy girl she couldn't bring herself to name.

She thought she could ignore the child growing inside her, that her life as the Hood didn't have to end.

She was wrong. It wasn't only the Hood who would disappear from Gaule, but Amalie Leroy as well. Would anyone mourn the daughter of a traitor, the sister of a traitor?

"They're all gone." Tears blurred her vision as a cough shook her chest.

"Who, Ames?" Tuck knelt beside her, gripping her hand. "Who is gone?"

"My father. My sister." She sucked in a breath, feeling it burn in her lungs. "Tyson."

Tuck shook his head. "Tyson is coming. He'll be here."

Each word was a struggle. "Shouldn't..." She took a short breath. "Have sent letter."

Tuck bowed his head. "Amalie, Tyson loves you. He'll be here."

Six months ago, she'd forced the man she loved to return to Bela. He'd fought for her, but she couldn't let him become involved in what she saw as her future. The life of an outlaw was not something one wished on the ones they loved. He hadn't seen it then, but she'd done it for him.

At the time, she didn't know of their child.

But now she was weak. In her final moments, she needed him. The burden she'd place on Tyson by allowing him to come was one she knew he'd accept. Especially after the letter she'd sent John to deliver begging Tyson to return to her. She told him of the child, but not her illness.

Tuck jumped to his feet as John burst into the room. "Is he with you?"

John fell to his knees at Amalie's bedside, and his eyes scanned her face. "I was so worried I'd be too late." He buried his face in her shoulder. "I love you, Amalie."

She attempted a smile as he lifted his face and placed a kiss on her forehead.

Tuck gripped John's shoulder and pulled him up. "Where is he?"

Amalie had seen despair many times before, but when John looked to her with glassy eyes, she knew the words he wanted to say. She'd never imagined silence could break her more than her failing body had.

"He didn't come," she rasped.

John shook his head. "I delivered the letter, but he would not return to Gaule."

She bit her lip to still its quivering and nodded. "Then I am ready."

"No, Ames." John pointed to the door. "I retrieved something better than Tyson Durand."

A caramel skinned young woman stepped from the shadows of the doorway. Candlelight lit her corkscrew curls.

"I know you." Amalie tried to push herself up, but failed.

"I am Maiya." The girl smiled.

The Draconian healer. Amalie's eyes widened. She'd taken Alexandre Durand to Maiya and her father when he suffered a curse. The Draconians had magic, but not that of the Belaens. Theirs was a prized healing power.

John moved out of the way to allow Maiya near the bed.

Maiya pulled a knife free of her belt and cut away the fabric of Amalie's tunic. She stopped when the skin just below Amalie's neck was exposed.

Amalie held her breath as Maiya placed her palms on the bared skin. After a moment where nothing happened, warmth seeped into Amalie, chasing the chill away. It spread down her chest, easing Amalie's breathing before attacking the pain in her lower abdomen. Amalie's skin buzzed with the power.

She'd spent many years in the Draconian war surrounded by those with magic in their blood, but she'd never experienced it for herself. She'd never felt as if it was a part of her.

In the moments after Tyson Durand broke her heart for the last time, she finally understood him. The magic was everything.

After a while, Maiya pulled her hands back, her chest heaving from the exertion. She wiped sweat from her eyes. "You will live Amalie, but you will remain weak for some time. My magic used your own body's energy to heal. Eventually, you will be whole."

When death comes, it is supposed to take you away from the pain of life. It's supposed to be unbeatable. Amalie had longed for the relief of death.

Worse than dying was being forced to live.

142

In the end, Tyson never came. But a dying girl sent that letter. Amalie Leroy grew weak in her final moments.

The Hood was her strength. That identity was all that mattered now. One of the maids entered the room holding a baby girl that could have no place in that world.

Amalie turned her face away. "Take her. Please." In order to protect the child, she had to let her go.

Present

Amalie threw her bow on the table as she entered her sitting room. Why did Tyson have to kiss her? She wanted to hate him, needed to hate him.

Yet, being that close to him, felt just as it had before. He was her family, once. Her whole world. Legally, he was still her husband. Practically, he was the man sent to arrest her.

And then there was Anders. She cursed as she poured a cup of wine. After taking a sip, she slammed the cup down. Burgundy liquid splashed over the sides, but she didn't care. None of it mattered anymore. Not her house or the damn estate.

Even her mission as the Hood seemed to be ending. Could she continue while the queen kept sending her people in search of a criminal? They already knew the Hood operated on her lands. How long would it be before they connected her to the outlaw?

"It was a trap," she growled before picking up her cup and chugging the rest of the wine. "A damn trap." Anger burned through her, and she hurled her empty cup against the wall before ripping the hood from her head and dropping it to the ground. She stomped back into the corridor and went in search of Tuck, finding him outside the barracks.

"How's Will?" She'd calmed enough to hide her anger.

"Lucky the wounds wasn't deep." Tuck ran a tired hand through his hair. "Edmund brought him back, and Maiya has tended his injury."

"Good, what of the others?"

"Cameron awaits orders. Do you want me to send for John as well?"

She considered that for a moment. Did she trust John after what he'd done to Ty? Should she care about what happened to Ty? John protected her with every breath he took... but he was unpredictable. She shook her head. "No. We fell into Anders' trap, and he is still a danger. We don't want to make contact. Tell Cameron to assign a watch to Anders for the duration of his time here. He'll know he's being watched so we must be careful he can't connect them to us here at the estate. Cam is to only use men from the forest, not those who also serve here. Send our guards to the forest instead. There are men to bury."

Tuck nodded and moved to walk away.

"Tuck," she called one final time.

He turned.

"Has Tyson returned yet?"

He dipped his head. "I'm sorry, Amalie. He has not."

She gestured for him to go before entering the barracks to check on Will. Where would Tyson have gone in the middle of the night? She tried not to worry that something happened to him, but worrying was part of who she was.

She'd always fear for those she cared about and despite all desire to stop, she cared about the prince.

Chapter

Twenty

Tyson knew he shouldn't return to the woods where the outlaws lived. There would be no warm welcome for a prince among thieves in the middle of the night.

The criminal who escaped his mother's death sentence had things to answer for.

The small huts they called home came into view in the middle of a clearing. No candles burned at this hour. Some of these men and women would be following Anders no doubt, but there was one Tyson hoped was home.

It was time they faced each other. Despite still being weak from using so much magic, the thought of facing John Little didn't frighten him. Tyson had confronted many worse people in his life.

He barely saw anything else as he made his way to John's home and slammed his heavy boot into the door. Wood splintered. He kicked again, and the roughly built door burst inward.

Tyson stood in the doorway, his chest heaving as John scrambled from his bed, a long knife in hand.

"What do you want, Prince?"

Tyson stepped forward, drawing his own blade. Blood from the guards he'd slain coated the steel. John's eyes flicked from the blood to Tyson and narrowed. "What have you done?"

Tyson glanced at the blade as if he hadn't noticed its state. The silver light made it shine. "I protected her." He didn't need to say who he meant.

John swallowed. "Please, tell me what has happened. Is she okay? Is that why you've come?"

The fear in John's eyes matched his own. "You're in love with her."

John swallowed but didn't respond.

Tyson advanced and knocked John's knife out of his grasp with a flick of his sword. He closed the remaining distance, his eyes wild, and lifted the blade to press the tip against John's chest. "Years ago, something happened to Amalie. She thinks things of me that are not true. You will tell me the truth." He gestured back to the bed with his sword. "Sit."

John lowered himself, never once taking his eyes from Tyson.

"Speak," Tyson ordered. He lowered his sword and dropped into a chair near the bed. While waiting for John to find the words, he lit the candle on the table beside him, bathing the small room in its orange glow.

John sighed. "You were never supposed to return."

"Why? Because of Amalie's mission as the Hood?"

John's eyes widened in surprise. "You know. Are you going to arrest her and take her to your mother?"

Tyson leaned forward against the hilt of his sword as he dug its tip into the dirt floor. He hadn't considered what any of this meant. His mind still couldn't grasp that the shy girl he fell in love with was now one of the kingdom's greatest outlaws. She must have known where Simon was this entire time. She'd lied and broken laws.

But the thought of watching her dangle from a noose stole every bit of life from his bones. No, just as he'd said to her, he would protect her even if it meant defying his mother.

"If I answer your question..." Tyson fixed his eyes on John. "Will you answer mine?"

John only nodded.

Tyson sighed. "Amalie is safe from me, but this night, one of my mother's most ruthless captains almost ensnared her."

John shot to his feet. "I must help her."

Tyson scowled. "Sit down, man. If she wanted you, she'd have sent for you. Amalie is fine."

John's eyes rested on the bloody sword again. "You killed your mother's men? For the Hood?"

"Make no mistake, John Little. Not every royal guard who comes through these parts is loyal to the queen. I know what you all think of her, but my orders were to bring the Hood in alive and find the guard who'd been abducted. The men who came tonight wanted the Hood dead. That was the captain's doing. If we are going to protect Amalie, we can't be trying to beat each other bloody at every opportunity."

John's shoulders dropped. "I'll do anything."

"I have answered your question, now I need the truth. Amalie claims I didn't come for her when she asked and somehow I know you were involved."

"I'll tell you, but I don't want you holding a sword while I do."

Tyson considered him for a moment before setting his sword aside. "I'm waiting."

John sighed. "Amalie was sick. We thought she was dying. She..." He squeezed his eyes shut as if the words hurt to say.

"She wanted you there... in the end. She sent me to Bela with a letter."

"I received no letter." Tyson crossed his arms over his chest, his hatred for the man before him making it hard to sit still.

"I know." John opened his eyes and fixed them on Tyson. "I was in the village in Bela, but couldn't do it. I couldn't give it to you. Amalie was no longer yours."

"That wasn't for you to decide," he growled.

"No." John shifted his eyes away. "It wasn't. When I made my decision and was preparing to leave, I met a young healer who claimed she could help."

"Maiya."

John nodded. "She returned to Gaule with me and saved Amalie's life."

"I should slit your throat, John Little." Anger burned through him, pulling his magic to the surface. "I should drown you right where you sit. You say you want what's best for Amalie, but you do not listen to her." An image of Amalie on her deathbed thinking Tyson refused to see her one last time nearly broke him. All her anger and hatred over the last couple years suddenly made sense. "You say she wasn't mine, and you're right. Amalie belongs to no man. She has her own mind, her own wishes, and she..."

She thought he'd abandoned her.

He'd broken her.

He lunged for John, wrapping his hands around the other man's throat. "She needed me," he yelled. Amalie no family left who loved her as he had. She wasn't accepted in noble circles or palace drawing rooms. She'd only had him. "How could you do that to her?"

John choked, trying to breathe. "She was dying."

John's grip on Tyson's arms weakened, and he sagged back on the bed. Tyson released him and fell away, sense returning in full force. Did he kill him? He watched with bated breath until John's chest rose and fell. Only unconscious.

Tyson burst from the house into the fresh air, gasping for breath. He wiped a hand across his face as a few others stepped from their homes, awakened by the commotion.

Tyson didn't spare one glance for them as he took off running through the trees. He had to get to her, to tell her she was wrong. That if he'd gotten the letter, he wouldn't have wasted a single second in coming for her. Not even La Dame could have stopped him.

By the time he made it back to the estate, dawn had thrown colors across the sky, lighting up the dark.

He knew his tired body wouldn't be able to rest, but the estate slept. He passed the guards and entered the great house where he ran into Tuck outside the hall.

Relief washed over Tuck's face. "You've returned. We've been worried. The village and the woods are not safe for the Prince of Gaule. Especially with guards roaming the streets tonight."

Tyson stopped in front of his old friend. "Tell me, Tuck, were you more worried about the guards finding me or Amalie's own people? Are they the sort to hurt a prince?"

The grimace flashing across Tuck's face was all the answer he needed. The Hood was considered a danger not only for the events she caused, but for the company she kept. The rumors hadn't gotten that wrong. How could Amalie believe in what she was doing while she consorted with such people? With thieves and murderers.

Tyson turned away from Tuck in disgust. He'd stormed into the house wanting to confront Amalie about everything John told him. Wanting her to know the truth. But maybe the truth would make no difference.

Tuck gripped his arm, holding him in place. "She's been waiting up for your return all night."

Those words stopped Tyson. Amalie said she no longer knew him. She said she didn't want him. But she still cared. That much was in her very being. It was who she was. Some of the anger he felt toward Tuck dissipated.

"Where is she?"

"Her father's hall."

Tyson reeled back. When he'd lived here with Amalie, she'd closed off the large room her father had used to meet with his people. She'd claimed too much wrong happened there. He'd taken advantage of his people, plotted against his king.

"Do you need me to show you the way?" Tuck asked.

Tyson shook his head. "I know this estate almost as much as I know my own home in Bela."

Tuck released him. "Just... Ty... Amalie tries to be strong. She's a proud woman. These last few years have changed her, but I still see glimpses of the girl who arrived at my door wanting to marry the man she loved."

"Thanks, Tuck." Tyson patted his shoulder. "You've been there for her when I couldn't. She doesn't think she needs anyone, but we all do. I'm glad she's had you."

Lord Leroy's hall lay at the far end of the estate. Two enormous carved mahogany doors marked the entrance. They usually sat locked, the room only a remnant of the long-dead ideals of a traitor.

Now, one door sat cracked open. Tyson gripped the cold iron handle and pulled it far enough to slip through. Darkness shrouded the room save for a single lit torch near the front, illuminating a wooden chair with lions carved into each arm and a girl sitting in it with her face in her hands and her back impossibly still.

The flicker of the light danced along her ornate purple

threaded gown and ivory skin. At the sound of the door closing, she jerked her head up.

She jumped from the chair, but then seemed to remember their current circumstances and sat back down. "I'm glad to see you've come back safely, your Highness."

Tyson took a tentative step forward. "I didn't expect to find you in here, Amalie."

A harsh laugh pushed past her lips. "Isn't this where all traitors belong?" She ran her hands along the arms of the chair, feeling each groove as if making them her own.

"You're not a traitor, Ames."

"Whatever you want to call me. Outlaw. Criminal. Fraud. The facts are the same. I'm betraying Gaule, betraying your mother. I kept her most trusted man captive in my household."

"You were desperate, Ames."

She shook her head. "My mind was clear. I made each decision. And do you know why we can't be together, Tyson?"

He shook his head, letting her speak.

"Because if I had to do it again, I'd do nothing different. This is who I am. I am my father's daughter."

"I don't believe that for one second."

She sighed. "It doesn't matter what you believe. Gaule will soon tire of their masked vigilante. They will turn on me as their villages and their homes are searched by the queen's men."

"I'll protect you."

Her lips drew down. "Have you forgotten our conversation already, Ty? You and I cannot be together. I'm sorry if that causes you pain. It was never my intention."

"You're wrong." He walked forward until he entered the circle of light and looked down into her tired eyes. "I never got your letter, Ames. John... he didn't bring it to me. I would have come for you. I would have done anything for you."

Her expression didn't change at his news. "Like I said, I'm sorry if this causes you pain-"

"Didn't you hear me?"

She studied him for a moment, her eyes glassing over. "I'm sorry to cause you pain."

"Stop saying that!"

"What would you like me to say, Tyson?"

He ran a hand through his dark hair. "That you love me. That you know how much I love you."

She closed her eyes, one tear escaping. "You think you know everything. Every reason. Every feeling. But you don't. Not even close. The Hood was not my biggest secret, Ty. Not from you. But you'll get no answers here. Like I said, I'm sorry to cause you pain."

Tyson took a step back. "That's it then? That's the end?"

She wiped away her tears and met his gaze. "That's the thing about this life, Tyson. Endings are inevitable."

Chapter

Twenty-One

The problem with allowing cracks to remain in one's heart was that eventually they widened. And one day, they'd be large enough to swallow a person whole.

Tyson had allowed Amalie to remain in his heart as a crack, as damage that had never been repaired. And now, she'd broken him wide open.

But she wasn't the only one.

He burst into Edmund's room, slamming the door open without knocking.

Edmund lay sprawled on top of the thick furs. He didn't wake.

Tyson threw his hand out toward a water pitcher on the table at the far side of the room. The clear fluid rose into the air before sailing across and dropping on Edmund's head.

He sputtered awake. "What in La Dame's name do you think you're doing?" He flicked wet hair out of his eyes. "Oh, let me guess. You tripped and your magic just fell out." He sat up. "Well, come on. Don't tell me you're out of power now."

Tyson curled his fingers, and the water drained from Edmund's hair and shirt until they looked as dry as they had before.

Edmund smiled, all tiredness fading from his face. "Good. Now tell me what has your knickers in a twist."

"How long have you known?" He huffed out a breath. When Edmund didn't respond, he stepped closer to the bed. "Dammit, man! I have been searching for the Hood for weeks now, planning to bring him to my mother. And it isn't even a him." He dropped into the chair near the bed. "Why didn't you tell me?"

Why didn't Edmund stop Tyson from letting himself hope again?

Edmund pushed himself up and swung his legs over the side of the bed. He shoved the blanket from his naked body, but Tyson barely noticed. All he could see were Amalie's eyes the moment she'd walked away from him. Pain. Years of pain. He'd caused every bit of it. He wanted to use every ounce of his magic on John for what he did, but he thought of everything Etta taught him.

The people of Gaule feared magic users because of what they could do to them. No matter Tyson's anger, he refused to be the monster they wanted him to be.

The monster Amalie would see him as.

She had secrets still, but she didn't trust him and that hurt worst of all.

Edmund scrubbed a hand over his face and sighed. "If you're going to wake me at such an hour, the least you can do is stop ogling me and fetch me my clothes."

Red crept up Tyson's neck to the tips of his ears as he realized his gaze had been directed Edmund's way, even though his mind focused on the girl he couldn't quite figure out. He averted his eyes before standing and walking to where Edmund's trousers hung on a peg on the wall. He tossed them to his friend and faced him once again when he was partially dressed. "No more stalling, Edmund. I want answers and you're the only one who can give them to me."

Edmund settled back onto his bed and studied him for a moment. "The hanging."

"What?" Tyson leaned forward.

"John's hanging. That was when I found out about Amalie. I still don't understand everything that went on that day, but I would guess Tuck did something to John when he performed his last rites. Then Amalie shot him and he appeared to die. I caught Amalie sneaking from a building in the village. That was when I knew."

Tyson shook his head. "All this time, I've questioned villagers and slept under Amalie's roof, and you've known she was the Hood?" Had everyone lied to him? Another thought struck him. "You didn't trust me. Neither of you did. I thought... Never mind what I thought. I was obviously wrong." He stood and made it to the door before Edmund called him back.

"What did you think, Ty?"

Tyson paused with his fingers wrapped around the handle. "My entire life, I felt out of place. The man who raised me held no love for me. My mother tried as best she could, but she lived in a kingdom that hated the magic inside me. My true father never claimed me. And my siblings... Alex always had you. I was envious for years because I never had that person in my life who'd do anything for me."

Edmund opened his mouth to speak but shut it when Tyson turned and pinned him with angry eyes.

"It's been years since I felt like that. Since I didn't know my place. Because I had you now and Etta and Alex. Even when I lost Amalie, you were there. I trusted you with everything." He rubbed the back of his neck and studied the floor. "This is big,

Edmund. The woman I still love with every bit of my soul is the outlaw I've been hunting." He lifted his eyes once more. "And my best friend let me. I don't know what to do with this, with any of it."

He pushed out a long breath. "I have to ask you a question I know you know the answer to. I can move past most of this eventually, Edmund, but not Simon. You know where he is, and I need you to tell me."

Edmund scrambled from the bed and crossed the room, meeting Tyson's gaze unflinchingly. Regret shone in his eyes, but he didn't voice it. There were no sorries that could fix what had broken inside Tyson. Nothing that could erase the fact that Edmund lied to him, deceived him. That Amalie broke them instead of just voicing her actions, her desires.

But what would Tyson have done? If she'd told him back then that she felt called to serve the people as a renowned criminal, would he have accepted it? Loved her anyway?

He didn't know the answers to his own questions, but Edmund's next words sliced through him.

"Simon is here."

Tyson sucked in a breath. "He's in the Leroy estate?" Right under his nose? Ty accepted this mission to find his mother's guard, but Simon was more than that. He'd been a friend to Tyson and an ally to Etta.

"Show me."

Edmund brushed past Tyson and pulled open the door without bothering to put on a tunic. His blonde hair fell in a mane about his shoulders, wild and unkempt.

Tyson ran a hand over his tired face, knowing he must look rough after a night of no sleep. Only servants roamed the halls at the early hour but as they turned into a corridor on the other side of the estate, four guards came into view.

Simon was in there. Tyson was sure of it.

He leaned close to Edmund, forgetting for a moment the chasm between them. "Does Amalie think those guards could overcome Simon?"

One corner of Edmund's mouth curved up. "Most people underestimate magic until it's in front of them."

Tyson straightened before facing the guards. If Simon was still here, it was because he'd chosen not to break free, not because they'd prevented his escape. Not even the illustrious Hood could hold a magic man with the strength of Simon.

The guards nodded to Edmund and Tyson narrowed his eyes. How often had his friend visited Simon and failed to mention it?

One of the armored men pushed open the door. The sight that greeted Tyson sent relief exploding through his every bone, every organ. He'd spent weeks worrying about Simon, thinking the guard was dead or worse.

Instead, his friend looked up from a chair in front of a roaring fire and paused with a china cup tilted against his lips. He lowered it and a smile spread across his face.

"Si." Tyson stumbled into the room until he stood in front of his mother's guard. "You're okay."

Simon set aside his tea and stood. "If you're here, I assume that means you know."

Tyson didn't have time to consider Simon's words before he lunged forward and wrapped his arms around his old friend.

A chuckle rumbled through Simon. "It's good to see you too, my prince."

Tyson pulled back, gripping Simon's upper arms in his large hands. "I wasn't sure we'd meet again." Some of the anger and the hurt he'd been feeling since the previous night loosened in his gut. He'd succeeded in his mission and could send Simon home to his mother—even if he didn't capture the Hood.

"Lady Leroy has been a gracious hostess."

Tyson released him and turned back to Edmund. "You may leave."

"Ty—" Edmund protested.

Tyson hardened his jaw. "If you're going to make decisions as if our friendship means little, I can as well. Edmund, I am the prince of both the kingdom you currently stand in and the one you call home. I've given you an order. Go. You aren't needed here."

Edmund's shoulders dropped as he gave a slight nod and turned to the door. Tyson didn't speak again until it shut behind him.

Simon lowered himself back into his chair. "I've never known you to be cruel, Tyson."

Tyson sighed and sank into a chair beside Simon, ignoring his comment. "They've kept you here this entire time. Amalie and her men. You're their prisoner."

Simon was quiet for a long moment. "I could leave this place any time I wanted to. You know that as well as I do."

"But Amalie—"

"Spent years around magic folk, including but not limited to you. She's not quite sure how powerful I am. I see the uncertainty in her eyes. But she knows her men can't keep me here. I could overpower them easily."

"Then why are you still here?" He leaned forward, resting his elbows on his knees and letting the fire warm his face.

Simon kept his eyes trained on the dancing flames. "Because the moment I'm free, I have a duty to return to your mother. To tell her everything I know. But not just her. I am bound to reveal my knowledge to her guards who now search for the hooded archer we call an outlaw." He shook his head. "I'm not ready for that burden. I'm not prepared to put Amalie at the mercy of Gaulean law."

Tyson turned his head to study his friend. He'd always

respected Simon, but the man was like no other. He always did what he thought was right, no matter the cost.

"So, for now, you're a prisoner."

He nodded and repeated the words. "For now, I'm a prisoner."

In a prison that couldn't hold him.

Tyson relaxed back into his chair as exhaustion washed over him. In only a day's time, everything he thought he knew had changed.

He closed his eyes, imagining the rolling hills of Bela. Etta once told him nothing good happened to a person when they crossed into Gaule. Maybe she was right. A few years ago, he'd imagined he could make a life here. He'd been wrong.

"I miss my nephew." The words tumbled out of his mouth, and he almost laughed at the mundane nature of them. Here he was with life altering secrets on his tongue, but Viktor pushed all the shadows from his mind.

Simon's eyes lit as if shining from within. "Etta has a child?"

Tyson nodded. "Viktor. When I left, she hadn't yet sent the royal birth announcement to foreign kingdoms, but I assume my mother knows by now that she has a grandson." His lips slanted up. "Edmund and Alex fight over who gets to hold him every time he wakes. One little baby has changed our entire world."

Simon laughed. "They have a tendency to do that."

Tyson didn't bring up his mother's pregnancy or the fact he knew Simon was the father. Instead, he spoke of home. Of his small house in the village. Of his family. In the years since leaving Amalie behind in Gaule, he hadn't considered himself happy. But now, as he caught Simon up on life in Bela, he realized he'd been wrong.

Amalie hadn't broken him.

She hadn't removed his heart from his body.

He'd gone on loving the family who awaited him back home.

"What are you going to do?" He met Simon's clear gaze.

They both knew he couldn't remain a prisoner forever. Not when he had a child coming and a queen to protect. "One of the guards keeping an eye on me is a man named Will."

Tyson nodded. He knew the man. The Madran mercenary Edmund had carried unconscious back to the estate only the night before.

Simon continued. "If Amalie continues as she has, it ends only with a noose around her neck. Will can get her to Madra where Queen Helena will protect her. As soon as they are gone, I will return to your mother."

It was a sound plan. Tyson knew Helena Rhodipus. She'd take care of Amalie better than anyone.

He rose from the chair and stuck out his hand. Simon grasped it.

"I assume I'll see you soon, my friend. With the royal births and the delays in foreign assemblies they've caused, there is bound to be a summit of kingdoms."

Simon released him. "You're leaving?"

Tyson nodded. "It's time I return home. Gaule holds too many ghosts for me now."

As soon as he was back in the hall, he froze. Edmund leaned against the opposite wall waiting for him.

"Are you going to say farewell to Amalie before you scamper away?" Edmund pushed off the wall.

Tyson brushed past him, sighing when Edmund's steps matched his own. "I'm not welcome here, Edmund."

"She needs you."

"No, she doesn't. Amalie will be safe as soon as she gets to Madra. She has many people she trusts far more than she trusts me, and they can get her on a ship. I do no good by causing her any more pain than I already have."

"This is bullshit." Edmund gripped Tyson's arm and pulled him to a stop. "I've thought it was this secret identity of hers keeping you two apart. She was afraid of revealing it to you. But you don't care about the Hood. I know you don't."

"Edmund, just because you've found the one man who can put up with you for all of eternity does not make you an expert on relationships, especially mine." He pulled his arm free.

"But you love her."

"I will always love Amalie Leroy. It is my curse. Something inside her is broken, and it's not something I can fix. Loving someone does not come easy for a Leroy, and it's a task she seems to find impossible. I don't think there's a single person in the six kingdoms she'd love more than her mission." He began walking again. "It's time I find something else to wish for in this life."

Edmund didn't follow him, but his voice echoed off the stone ceilings. "I've never known you to give up, Tyson Durand."

Tysons turned to Edmund one final time. "It is not giving up to accept defeat, my friend. It is growing up."

Tyson collected his belongings from his room, his eyes scanning the familiar walls. When he'd arrived, he planned to arrest the Hood once he discovered the outlaw's identity. Amalie had known why he was here and invited him to stay anyway. She'd willingly brought her would-be pursuer into her home.

He might never know her reasoning, but he'd never forget these last few weeks with her. Even as she hated him, being near her gave him a sense of peace he'd lacked these last few years. But that was gone now as he stood like a stranger inside those walls.

When he arrived in the courtyard, it surprised him to see

Edmund standing with their horses. He shouldn't have been surprised. Edmund had come with him to Gaule in the first place, but he didn't know where they stood. So many lies rested between them now.

Edmund smiled. "You didn't think I'd let you leave without me, did you?"

Tyson ran a hand down his horse's soft nose. "I never know what you'll do, Edmund."

Edmund's face pinched in pain. "Look, Ty, I'm sorry. I should have told you. You deserved honesty from me."

Tyson sighed and tied his bag and sword to the saddle. "I know Etta asked you to accompany me. But, Edmund, I'm not any less capable than you or my sister or brother."

"Of course you aren't."

"Then you need to stop treating me like it." He hauled himself into the saddle and nudged the horse around.

"I can do that." He paused. "I bid adieu to Amalie for both of us. She wished us well and said she will miss our presence in her house."

Tyson sighed. "No she didn't."

Edmund laughed. "Well, she did say she wished us safety on the road." He coughed and lowered his voice. "And that it was about time we left them in peace."

"That sounds more like her." Tyson gripped the reins in one hand and kicked his heels to take off through the open gates.

His mother would forgive him for not going back to the palace since Simon would return to her. That was all she'd wanted from this mission. And Ty wouldn't feel better until he set foot in Bela once more. Until he sat with his sister and looked into the innocent eyes of his nephew. Eyes that had yet to see how cruel the world could be. He had a heart that had yet to be broken and a mind that had yet to be filled with falsehoods.

Edmund pulled his horse up beside Tyson. "Do you think Viktor will remember me?"

"He's a baby," Tyson deadpanned.

"Yes." Edmund scratched his jaw, deep in thought. "But that's not what I asked. Will he remember me? Or has Alex stolen him."

Tyson laughed. "You realize Alex is his father, right?"

Edmund waved a hand. "That doesn't matter. Kids like their uncles better, anyway. I hated my own father so there's still time for me to win Viktor's loyalty."

Leave it to Edmund to make Tyson smile when he'd thought that impossible. "It's not a competition, Edmund. And you shouldn't want Viktor to love you more than his own father."

"It's not like it'll be hard. Alex is so... Alex."

"That's the king of Bela and my brother you're speaking of." Tyson suppressed his grin. "Have some respect. Besides, the kid will be smart enough to love his Uncle Tyson more than both of you."

Edmund sighed. "You're right. I didn't take pity into account. Pity love is stronger than awesome Uncle Edmund love."

Tyson reached over and shoved Edmund. The blonde giant pretended to tilt from his horse before righting himself. "Violence is mean," he grumbled.

"Says the best swordsman in both Gaule and Bela."

Edmund shrugged. "Someone has to protect you."

Tyson tried to push him again, but Edmund kicked his heels and cantered through the village. They reached the paths that would take them from the busy streets into the rolling countryside. The nearest village was half a day's ride away, but they wouldn't enter it. The people of Gaule were no longer theirs.

Both Tyson and Edmund had grown up in the kingdom they were so desperate to be rid of. Neither had been accepted for who they were. Both wore the revelations of their pasts like armor protecting them from the memories.

Tyson glanced back at where the estate walls rose above the rest, seeing it one final time. He didn't plan on returning. He'd still see his mother on her royal visits to Bela, and he loved her, but Amalie was the final string tying him to Gaule. Now that it had been cut, there was nothing left for him but pain.

With a shake of his head, he left the village behind, hoping one day it would get easier. That one day, he wouldn't miss the love of his life, the most important part of his childhood. That he could eventually forgive Amalie for breaking them.

Chapter
Twenty-Two

Cold seeped into Amalie's bones as she walked the halls of her seemingly empty estate. In truth, people surrounded her. Guards. Maids. Cooks.

And Tuck. He caught up to her, but she didn't slow. Continuing to move was the only way to keep the ice from freezing her entirely.

"Just say it, Tuck." She pulled her chestnut hair over one shoulder, weaving her fingers through the strands.

"Tyson and Edmund left. One of the servants brought the matter to me. I then questioned the stable lads and guards at the gate. They rode out early this morning."

She'd known. Edmund had wished her well before leaving, but even before that, her conversation with Tyson in the early hours of the morning had the distinct feel of finality to it.

She wouldn't see Tyson again. She'd pushed him away so even the most loyal man Gaule had ever seen would leave her behind. For good this time.

She thought over his words. He hadn't known. He could

have been lying, but the rational part of her knew Ty would never lie like that, not to her.

John, on the other hand... She couldn't even muster up the anger necessary to confront her oldest friend. As she considered why, the reason became obvious. John's betrayal didn't surprise her. He'd trained her, taught her everything she knew. He'd created the mission she now called her own.

But he'd always done what he wanted. For years, she kept a careful eye on him during raids, for fear he would harm the waggoneers and traders. The night she'd help him escape his cell was forever implanted into her mind. The way he killed effortlessly when anyone got in his way.

For the first time, she truly considered the men who claimed complete loyalty to her. They protected her, sure. They helped the people of the village. But they didn't operate on the same level of morality as she did.

And she'd unleashed them on Gaule. She'd trained them to take up the mantle. Told them they were noble in their actions.

The mission couldn't change who they were.

It couldn't make John any more honest. Any more true.

He'd kept Tyson from her in the weakest moment of her life. At a time when she'd needed him. Maybe if Ty had come, she wouldn't have given up her child. Maybe strangers wouldn't be raising a little girl who was in constant danger just because of who her mother was.

If anyone ever found out the Hood's identity... that was why Amalie played in the shadows instead of giving the people a face of hope.

"Ames." Tuck took her elbow and pulled her to a stop. "You need to talk to me."

"Why?" She lifted her eyes to his. "What about any of this requires words? They're gone. John deceived me. My mission is..." She sagged against the wall. "It's all over, Tuck. I can't keep

Simon here. The queen will soon know who I am. How am I to continue then?"

Tuck bent his neck to peer into her face. "The Hood is not who you are, Amalie."

"What if I can't be anything else?" She shook her head. "What am I supposed to do? I'm not a lady of court." She ran a hand over the deep purple gown that fit her like a second skin she wanted to shed. "These dresses are no more who I am than that hood."

"What is it about you people thinking your station in life has anything to do with who you are?"

"You people?" She pushed away from the wall.

He took a step back. "Those born into a life of titles and duties know nothing of life outside those bonds. I grew up in a village where the people had little. Their lives comprised working the same job every day to put food into their children's mouths. They didn't try to save the world or even leave their little corner of it. Yet, they had lives just as big, just as important as yours."

"What about you?" she asked, crossing her arms over her chest. "You left your village to join this mission. It's part of you as well."

He shook his head. "I am a part of it, but it has never been part of me. Do you want to know what I'm made of? It isn't noble duties or grand adventures. Inside me exists every single person I have loved in my life. They make up who I am. So, Amalie Leroy, you are a part of me, but your hood never has been."

His words struck Amalie, taking all the air from her lungs as she imagined Tyson stealing away with a part of her. The cold intensified until she could barely feel anything at all.

Tuck wrapped an arm around her shoulders. "There's still time to get him back."

She shook her head. "I've done so many unforgiveable things in the name of the Hood. I don't know how to be the woman he loved anymore."

Tuck squeezed her against his side. "You don't have to be her, Amalie. Maybe the real you is somewhere between the old and the new. Let Tyson grow to love her."

She peered up at him. He'd only been part of her life for a few short years, but Tuck was the closest thing to family she'd had other than Tyson. The love she felt for him was different, but no less true. There was nothing romantic about her feelings as she said, "I love you too, you know."

He smiled. "Good. Because you and I are a pair, Ames. I'll follow you anywhere. Even to Madra if that's where you want to go."

Footsteps sounded against the stone, breaking them from their conversation. Will rushed toward them.

Amalie met him halfway. "You're still recovering, Will. You shouldn't be out of bed."

Before he could respond, Maiya joined them in the hall. Amalie looked between the frightened expressions on both their faces.

"What has happened?" Tuck asked.

Will swallowed. "Captain Anders. He knows."

"He knows?" The ice in Amalie's veins thawed as fire raged inside her. "About what?" But she already knew the answer.

"John arrived here only minutes ago. He told us Caldon is gone. His smithy has been closed up and they don't think he's coming back."

The town blacksmith, Caldon, knew everything. He kept a room in the back of his shop for the Hood and her people to meet. And he'd accompanied Tuck's sister and her husband as they returned to their village with a new child they promised to keep safe.

If Caldon had left town... "He told the captain everything, didn't he?"

Will looked to Maiya. She cleared her throat. "We don't believe he revealed your identity because you would already be in chains if he had. But there are other secrets Caldon held." He paused for a moment. "A few people in the village reported Caldon buying supplies this morning with gold coins instead of on credit."

"Gold?" Tuck cursed. Gold coins weren't often seen in the poor villages of Gaule. Silver yes, bronze even. Never gold.

"And that is not the worst of it."

Amalie kept her gaze on the healer, watching her irises shine orange in the candlelight. "Tell me."

Will flicked his eyes from Tuck to Amalie in hesitation. "Captain Anders and his men have left town as well."

Amalie took off down the hall. The others followed her. "We have to leave. There is only one place Anders would go after speaking to Caldon. Cal might not have told Anders who I am, but he said enough to show the captain exactly how to draw me out. We make for the border village as soon as we can. Tuck, I need you to ready the horses. The three of you will accompany me. We don't have time to summon the rest of the men. Tell John to meet me in my rooms."

"John left, my lady." Will's strides matched hers.

Amalie halted. "What do you mean he left?" He would have known exactly what this meant. Even when things were bad between them, she wanted to believe he'd be there for her. Maybe she was wrong.

After everything she'd done for him, he let her down again. But there was someone in the estate who would help.

"Fine." She turned in the opposite direction. "Forget John, but make haste in preparing everything else. I'll meet you all in the courtyard."

They broke off from her path, but she didn't stop until she was outside a familiar door. The guards opened it for her.

"Simon." She stepped in. "I need you."

He rose from his chair. "Amalie, what's wrong? What has happened?"

"Captain Anders will find my daughter. I can't let harm come to her."

Surprise flickered across his face.

"Will you help me?"

He hesitated for only a moment before stepping forward and placing a hand on each of her shoulders. "How long of a head start does he have?"

"Only hours."

He squeezed. "Then we don't have time to waste."

The breath she'd been holding expelled from her lungs, and her shoulders dropped in relief. "Thank you. I—"

Simon released her. "There will be time for us to talk on the way, Amalie. We must leave."

She nodded and walked back into the hall. The guards followed them to her room to gather her bow and then to the courtyard where a dozen men lingered.

She sucked in a breath. "What is this?"

Tuck appeared at her side. "Word of what has happened traveled through the barracks. All those who are not needed to guard the estate have decided to come."

Tears sprang to her eyes as she looked over her men. These were not the criminals of the woods, but the simple villagers she'd raised up and trained. Some, she'd known most of her life.

Will led her horse forward. "We're with you, Amalie."

Tuck eyed Simon. "Are you sure about him, Ames? You've kept him prisoner. How do you know he won't turn on us as soon as we set him free?"

She turned to her friend. "Because... Simon is better than

me. And because he can't go back to the palace and tell the queen he didn't do everything in his power to save her grand-daughter."

"Captain Anders is a queen's man too. Won't he want to bring the girl to her?" one of her men asked.

Amalie shook her head. "Anders doesn't know who the child's father is. He only knows her mother is the Hood. If he knew my identity, he wouldn't bother going after the child. He'd come for me."

She stepped into the stirrup and swung her leg over her horse. "I don't know what the captain is planning. All I know is we'll be walking into a trap. I want to say I can't ask any of you to venture into the trap with me, but I'm too selfish. I'm not any kind of mother, but I have to save her. I need to." She glanced to Tuck, remembering his words. She wasn't made of the missions she undertook, but the people she loved. "My daughter is part of me."

Tuck placed a hand on her leg. "We're with you."

As she rode out into the village with her people at her back, she envisioned Tyson sitting beside her. He didn't know of the girl, but he'd have loved her with everything he had. "I'm going to save her, Ty," she whispered. "Anders won't use her as a pawn. And then maybe one day, she can be part of you too."

Chapter

Twenty-Three

Tyson cursed as he bent to examine his horse's leg. After galloping through the woods, his horse threw a shoe when he tripped over a dip in the path. Tyson should have seen it coming, but he wasn't paying attention.

Edmund slid down from his horse.

"Vérité would have jumped that on instinct." Tyson straightened and turned away from the horse.

"No, he would have sent you tumbling off just for the pure pleasure of it."

Tyson shook his head. Etta's horse was more human than many actual humans Tyson had met in his life. He protected the Belaen queen with his life. And this horse was no Vérité. "This beast won't be getting anywhere fast. We're almost to the next village. Let's camp here for the night and in the morning, we'll find a new horse at one of the farms outside the village."

"Good plan." Edmund unbuckled his horse's saddle. "I'm starving, anyway."

They made quick work of setting up camp as the sun hung

low over the trees. They had time left before darkness descended.

The horses drank from a small pond Tyson created with his magic. This wasn't how he expected the journey to go, but it seemed as if something was trying to keep him from leaving Gaule.

The endless roads winding down through the countryside and into the woods only made home feel farther away. Was it just that morning they left the Leroy estate?

He couldn't remember the last time he'd had a decent night's rest, or a decent meal for that matter. When Edmund held out an apple, Tyson took it and sank his teeth into the hard flesh without tasting it.

Edmund stood and began preparations for a fire to keep the chill from overcoming them in the night. They'd spent many nights together like this. First, when Etta was arrested in Gaule. She'd smuggled both Edmund and Tyson out of the magic-hating palace only to be found by Alex's men and taken back.

Tyson had been a mess leaving his home for the first time, but it opened an entirely new world for him.

And it solidified the bond between him and Edmund. Sitting in the woods with him held a familiar comfort. They were in it together. He could even forget the lies that got them here.

"Is it weird," Tyson began. "To have someone waiting for you back home?"

"Estevan?" Edmund sat down again as the fledgling flames flickered before them. He pushed air toward them with his power and they grew. He smiled. "I'm getting used to it. He's... everything."

There was a time when Tyson knew how that felt. "I hope you never lose that."

Edmund's smile faltered. "Ty, I almost did. We all thought

Stev was dead for months. But just because I no longer had him, it didn't mean I lost him. He was always with me."

"Because he never gave up on you."

Edmund shook his head. "He gave up on himself. He let them take him so the rest of us could get away. It took me a long time to forgive him for that."

"He had good reasons to let you go."

"Ty..." Edmund sighed. "Have you ever thought Amalie made the choices she has to protect you?"

"Protect me? No. Protect her mission? Maybe." His magic rose with his anger and he curled his fists to hold it back. It burned through his blood, drawing water from the ground. "She hates me because of the position I was born in to." His power pulsed. "Because my mother dares to hunt down criminals in her own kingdom." His hands shook until finally his magic broke free, dousing the small flames in water.

Edmund sighed. "That was stupid."

"I know." Tyson rubbed weak hands over his face. "I'm sorry. I don't know what to do anymore. I don't want to go on living like I have for the past couple of years."

"Then don't."

"That easy, huh?"

"No. None of this is easy. It's going to take time, but you'll be okay. And you're wrong, you know."

"I've been wrong about a lot of things." Tyson stared at the now soaking logs. "You'll need to be more specific."

Edmund sat forward, forcing Tyson to meet his gaze. "You asked me what it felt like to have someone to go home to, but you forget who we are, Ty. Estevan is there, yes, but Bela holds so much more for both of us. Amalie isn't there. She may never be there. But Alex and Etta are. They wait for us with little Viktor ready to make his uncles forget all about Gaule. We're a family, Ty. And we'll get you through this."

Edmund leaned back on his elbows. "Now, you've ruined our fire. Go find some dry brush to make a new one."

Tyson got to his feet and walked past the horses. Dusk was upon them now, but it wasn't yet too dark to see. He was bent over, picking up sticks and branches when he heard it. The muffled clop of a horse's hooves on the forest floor.

Dropping the sticks he'd gathered, he sprinted back to where he'd left Edmund and went straight to his pack. His bow lay on the ground beside it.

Edmund was on his feet before Tyson picked up the bow. "What is it?"

"A rider." Tyson wrapped his fingers around the smooth wood and knocked an arrow.

Edmund retrieved his sword. "How many?"

"I only counted one." It made no sense. Bandits traveled Gaule in roving packs. It was even too dangerous on the roads for them. Queen's guards wouldn't stray from their units, and the woods were no place for ordinary citizens.

Tyson crouched low behind a tree as the horse walked into their clearing. He lifted his bow and pulled the string back, releasing it quickly. The arrow sailed over top of the horse's head, missing the rider. A warning shot.

The horse reared back, and it took a moment for the rider to regain control. He pushed back his hood and scanned the trees.

"Tyson," he bellowed. "I'm not going to hurt you."

Recognizing the voice, Tyson met Edmund's gaze. John Little was the last person he trusted. The last person he wanted to associate with.

"Tyson." John turned his horse, still searching the trees. "Please." The desperation in his voice was not something Tyson expected from him. "Amalie needs you."

At those words, Tyson lowered his bow. If there was one

thing both he and John wanted more than anything, it was to protect Amalie.

But she hadn't wanted his protection anymore.

He stepped from the trees. John's face relaxed as soon as he saw him.

Edmund revealed himself with a scoff and slid his sword into its scabbard. "As if you could hurt us, criminal."

Tyson ignored him. "How did you find us?"

"This is the swiftest route to Bela for those who wish to stay off the main roads. I took a chance you wouldn't want to be seen." His hands relaxed on the reins. "We don't have time for distrust or idle chat. Amalie has left for a town near the Draconian border."

Tyson shrugged. "The border is no longer the danger it once was. In fact, Dracon is probably safer than Gaule. If she wishes to hide there instead of taking ship to Madra, she won't be found."

John shook his head. "You don't understand. She didn't go there to hide, and the village will be crawling with royal guards." His eyes danced from Tyson to Edmund. "It's a trap, and she's willingly walking in to it."

Worry sliced through Tyson. "Why would she do that?"

John's lips pressed into a thin line as he hesitated. "I cannot tell you that. I know you and I will never be allies. I can't imagine what you must think of me. But all I've ever wanted to do is protect my oldest friend. In that, you and I are the same. I know what loving Amalie Leroy feels like. That's why I know you will come with me. You will show up for her whether she returns your love or not."

"I..." Tyson opened his mouth and then shut it with a sigh. Amalie had been putting herself in danger for years, and he knew nothing of it. Why would John come to him now? He sighed. Did it matter? Amalie was in danger. As angry as he was at her, he'd still come when she called.

Edmund put a hand on his shoulder. "Whatever you decide, I'm with you."

Tyson nodded, swallowing the thickness in his throat. "There's nothing to decide, Edmund. It's Amalie."

He patted Tyson's back. "It's Amalie."

Tyson glanced toward his horse. "I'll need a new ride."

John nodded. "Come. There's a farm near here. The woman who runs it has given aid to the Hood before. She will help us."

Tyson and Edmund saddled their horses and mounted them. It was slow going when his horse couldn't even cantor, and by the time they came upon the patchwork crops, only the sliver of moon lit their path.

The woman was as accommodating as John promised and before long, the three men were racing across open ground, hoping they weren't too late to make a difference.

Chapter

Twenty-Four

It took three days to get to the small border town where too many memories lived. Amalie sat on the edge of their camp as dawn streaked across the sky. Behind her, the men and women who'd come to help roused themselves.

She closed her eyes, imagining the last time she'd set foot in the area. She hadn't been able to stay away like she knew she should have. Only a month after giving her daughter to Tuck's sister to keep safe, she'd found herself crouching on a rooftop that looked down into a courtyard surrounded by small homes.

The wail of a baby pierced the air moments before a petite woman with honey blonde hair stepped from the house. The bundle in her arms wiggled and Amalie held her breath.

"Hush," the woman cooed. "I'm not sure what's wrong with you today, baby girl, but momma needs a bit of quiet."

Amalie scooted forward to peer over the curved terracotta roof. A tile broke free, tumbling over the edge before crashing into the stone below.

Amalie cursed herself and scrambled backward, but it was too late. Sara glanced up, her eyes finding Amalie's hiding spot.

"You can come down, my lady." Her voice sounded tired, but not unkind.

Amalie only hesitated a moment before straightening and walking across the roof to the side where she climbed down the uneven stones jutting from the building. Once in the courtyard, she approached Sara.

"Does my brother know you're here?" the woman asked.

Amalie shook her head. "I received a summons to the royal palace. Tuck thinks I have obeyed and journeyed there."

"You've come all this way alone?"

"Yes." She didn't tell her John waited on the opposite roof, his bow at the ready in case anyone followed them.

Sara nodded, not questioning the woman who'd given up her own daughter. She pushed back the blanket, revealing the child who stopped crying as soon as her eyes fell on Amalie.

As if some forced tugged at her, Amalie stepped forward, needing to see more.

"This is Elayne." Sara smiled.

"Light," Amalie whispered. "Her name means light."

Sara nodded. "We never thought we'd have a child of our own, but she's been like a light illuminating this dark world."

A tear fell down Amalie's face. "It's perfect." She reached forward, but then pulled her hand back.

"We call her El."

Amalie wiped her face. "Hi El. I'm your... I'm a friend." She leaned down, taking in every feature from the chubby cheeks to dimpled chin. "I'm going to keep you safe. I promise you that."

A door opened behind them and Amalie turned to see Sara's husband Ayden walk out, arms crossed over his chest. "You shouldn't be here, lady Amalie." He stepped farther into the *courtyard. "You need to leave and never come back. For the child's sake as well as your own. It isn't safe."*

She nodded, hearing the truth in his words. It would never be safe for El as long as Amalie remained attached. She turned back to the baby and placed one hand on her head. She said nothing, but the child's eyes found hers, boring into her soul.

Ayden cleared his throat and Amalie pulled her hand back. She ran to the edge of the courtyard and pulled herself back onto the low roof. John joined her seconds later. As she sprinted away, a ghost in the night, her daughter's cry ripped through her.

She didn't let herself stop moving, stop widening the distance between them even as every bone in her body bid her to turn back.

A hand landed on Amalie's shoulder, jerking her from the memory. She wiped the back of her hand across her eyes before turning to Tuck.

"Will has returned." He nodded to where Will and the men who'd accompanied him into the village dismounted.

Straightening from her crouch, she crossed the leaf covered path. Her breath swirled in front of her face in the cool morning air, but she didn't feel the chill as impatience burned within her.

"Report." She stopped in front of Will.

Will met her gaze. "They're here. Hidden, but here. We saw a few guards disguised as villagers entering the house and then leaving. There was no sign of the child or her parents."

Amalie lifted her eyes to the gray sky, wishing for clarity. "They don't have them. If they did, they'd be causing such a scene it would be sure to get back to me. The fact that they're trying to blend in means they're searching for them."

Tuck joined them, Simon at his side. "Then there's only one place they could be."

She nodded, taking in Will's confused expression. "We had a plan in place in the event someone ever came for her." She lifted her voice. "We go in on foot. Leave a few men here with the horses. We don't want to cause a stir by thundering through the village."

A clamor of activity sounded behind her as her people gathered what they needed and readied themselves, but Amalie paid attention to none of it. All she saw were the edges of the village. Somewhere in that maze of homes, was a little girl she'd made a promise to.

"I'm coming, El." A drop of rain hit her cheek and then another. By the time they marched across the marshy ground, the skies opened, sending a torrent of angry tears.

Thunder split the world in two, as if ripping it at the seams and opening a gully inside each of them.

Muddy fields turned to crooked streets. This village had seen much destruction during the war with La Dame. It had once been protected by wards as all of Gaule had been. Once those fell with the death of their creator, magic folk and non fought in the streets, each trying to claim the kingdom for their own.

Tensions still ran high, but most magic folk had long since abandoned the damaged town for the safety of Bela.

They turned off the brick path and onto a dirt road that wound up toward the small abandoned house on the hill overlooking town. This village was a part of the Caron lands, but one of his lesser nobles presided over it. It was forgotten, ignored by the rest of Gaule, which had made it the safest place for El. An ignored village that may as well have been part of Dracon. A feared town where evil had once happened.

A small chapel stood ahead. A place Amalie knew well. It was where Tuck had once performed the ritual tying Tyson and Amalie together as husband and wife. Now, she hoped it protected the fruit of that union.

She motioned her people to spread out along the street.

They knew how to blend in. She approached cautiously and pulled open the partially damaged chapel door. Inside, pews lined each side leading up to an altar in the front. Disuse was clear in the dirt covered floor. Amalie walked forward and ran a finger along the dusty golden surface of the altar.

Tuck sighed behind her. "They haven't had a friar in residence since I left years ago." Regret rang in his voice.

"It wasn't your duty to stay when you yearned for more." She turned back to face him. "Come." Her eyes traced the footsteps near the far wall. "They're here."

Tuck lifted the heavy wood over a staircase hidden at the back of the room, and they descended into the dark cellar.

A man screamed as he ran at them with a short blade glinting in the candlelight. Amalie twisted out of the way moments before the clash of blades reached her ears.

"Ayden," Tuck grunted, pushing him back. "It's me."

Ayden dropped his sword, the steel crashing against the packed dirt floor. "Tuck?"

"It's me."

Ayden shrank back against the wall, his chest rising and falling rapidly.

Amalie approached him and surprised flashed in his eyes as recognition set in. "My lady?"

"Where are Sara and El?"

"Here, my lady." Sara stepped forward into the light of the single torch hanging on the wall.

She pulled a young girl behind her and the tension Amalie had felt since hearing they were in danger eased.

Dark curls framed a wide face. Some of the chubbiness was gone, but the dimple in her chin remained.

Sara's voice snapped Amalie out of her trance. "What is happening out there?"

Amalie took her hand and led her to the wall before sliding

down to sit, her legs unable to hold her up any longer. "You tell us. When my people didn't find you at your house, I knew you'd be here, but we only just arrived. What can you tell us?"

Sara clasped her shaking hands around El's waist and drew the girl into her lap before resting her chin on the child's head. "Ayden has been getting work at a farm. He walks there each day. Yesterday, on his way home, he noticed men he'd never seen before. They were talking to villagers, asking questions about a child. We knew they searched for our El so we escaped with only what we could carry."

Amalie nodded. "They're at your house now. We need to get you out of this village and to safety."

"Safety?" Ayden scoffed. "There is nowhere in Gaule safe for El. It was only a matter of time. They will always come for her because of who you choose to be."

"Ayden." Sara sighed.

"No." He narrowed his eyes. "She puts us in danger with every mission she embarks on. What would you have us do? We will protect our daughter with everything we have." Amalie didn't miss the emphasis he placed on the word *our*. "But what can we do against the royal guard?"

Amalie climbed to her feet to meet his gaze. "I will make this right. I will protect her."

His eyes blazed, but he turned away. That would have to be enough for now. El slipped from her mother's lap and waddled across to Amalie before lifting her arms.

In a simple world, Amalie could have picked her up. She could have told her she loved her or that not a day passed when she didn't think of her.

That she wondered if every choice in her life had been the wrong one.

Instead, she turned and walked to the stairs, stopping when she reached them. "I'm sorry. You won't be able to return home for any belongings. We will get you everything you need. Tuck and a few loyal men will get you to Bela."

"Bela." Ayden's tone had gone from angry to resigned.

Amalie nodded. "Go to the queen there and tell them everything." She squeezed her eyes shut. "El's father will protect you."

She didn't wait for the surprised questions she knew followed her. Instead, she climbed the stairs. Tuck and Simon would be able to help them. Etta and Tyson would protect them.

And he'd know.

As if the secret were already revealed, she could feel his hatred slither along her skin. Her life as the Hood was over as soon as Simon returned to the palace. But she wouldn't be welcome in Bela.

Tuck followed her out. "So, I'm to go to Bela?"

She nodded. "You must keep them safe. I trust no one else. Then... I want you to stay with them."

"Will you join us?"

She shook her head.

"I won't leave you, Ames. I'll get them settled and then join you wherever you are. I've told you before, I believe in you. My loyalty is yours and yours alone."

She gripped his hand. "I will leave that decision to you. Will and I are taking ship to Madra where the queen will welcome us. Most of the merry men will remain behind to care for the people of the village, but the Hood is too polarizing a figure to do much good anymore."

He squeezed her hand. "We will see each other soon."

She nodded, wishing she believed his words. "You need to leave. Get them out of here. You know the way through the back alley. I will stay long enough for you to get away. The rest of us can hold off any pursuit." She walked toward the chapel door to signal her people who waited concealed.

But as she stepped outside, the silence struck her. Her eyes darted to the rooftops and then the alley up ahead. No one was there.

"Simon," she whispered. "Come with me." She pushed Tuck back inside. "Bar the door. Don't open it unless you're sure it's me."

His eyes held an argument, but he only nodded and shut the doors, leaving Amalie and Simon standing alone on a deserted road.

"They won't hurt you, Simon, will they?" She glanced sideways at him.

He grimaced. "I'd like to think Anders won't, but he has little control over the men he commands."

That was news to her. She'd always attributed every atrocity she'd witnessed by his men to him, assumed they'd been following orders. She'd known the captain a long time. He was fiercely loyal to the throne of Gaule, but he operated under no moral code. He'd do whatever he thought was needed to keep them safe.

Even if it meant taking a child as a bargaining chip to draw out the notorious outlaw.

Amalie calmed her breathing and pulled her hood up around her head. Her fingers flexed on her bow as Simon drew his sword. They walked down the steps and crossed the street, the only sound was the patter of rain hitting the dirt, turning it to mud.

Amalie paused as a thought came to her. "Where are all the people who live here?" Her eyes darted to the buildings on either side. No movement at windows. Not a sound of a closing door. Nothing.

Simon spoke the words she'd been thinking. "They're gone."

She lowered her voice. "We feared a trap at Sara and Ayden's house, but they never expected us there." She shook her head. "Calden." He'd even revealed this plan to Anders.

Before another thought came to her mind, shouting drew her eyes to the far end of the street where horses barreled toward them. Armored men poured from the alleys and appeared on rooftops, their bows drawn.

Amalie's heart thudded in her chest, but she dared not lift her bow. She widened her stance and lifted her chin to meet the eyes of the man riding through the center of the throng. Anders couldn't see her face underneath her hood, but she could see his, eyes blazing in triumph.

Simon lowered his weapon and stepped forward. "Captain."

Anders sneered. "Look here, men. Simon, the great protector of Queen Catrine has allied himself with the Hood." He leaned down. "We've been searching the kingdom for you, magic man."

The venom in his voice wasn't new. There was a time when Anders was the top guard for the king, commanding men from the comfort of the palace. But Catrine hadn't wanted him involved in her reign so she sent him to a roving unit, meant to keep peace in Gaule.

All they did was terrorize the kingdom instead.

The guards lined up in a half circle around their new prisoners as Anders jumped down, his feet crashing into a puddle. He splashed his way forward, flicking rain out of his face.

Amalie no longer cared what happened to her. The person she loved most in the world was hidden in the chapel behind her, and she'd do whatever she needed to keep the promise she'd made. She would protect her.

She would save her.

Simon's muscles flexed as he prepared to use his magic to fight. But Amalie knew even he could not take on so many men.

She placed a hand on his arm just long enough to feel him relax. And then she did the only thing she could.

Her fingers shook as she gripped the edges of her hood. "I am who you want." She lifted her voice. "I am the Hood." She pushed the heavy fabric off her head and raised her gaze.

Captain Anders froze as a slow smile spread across his face. "This is a surprise. I imagined it was one of your guards. How do we know this isn't a ruse? That the real Hood isn't getting away as we speak?"

She shook water out of her eyes and raised her bow, knocking the arrow and drawing the string in one fluid motion. Before anyone could react, the tip of the arrow was embedded in the thigh of one of the men hidden in a nearby alley. He howled in pain and dropped to the ground.

"You've underestimated me because I was a lady of the court." She lowered her bow. "It protected me once, but I suspect it will protect me no more. I will come with you, Captain. Under one condition."

"You are in no position to be making demands."

She scowled. "Release my people. I know you've taken them." She'd expected a dozen to be waiting for her.

"I have done no such thing."

"Lies no longer do us any good." She lifted a brow, trying to quell the fear blossoming in her chest. "You want the Hood. I understand that, Captain. But I knew you once, and I don't believe you want to kill my people. At least not without questioning them. You're holding them in case I didn't appear."

Anders studied her for a moment before turning away. "Take them both into custody. Then search the chapel."

"No." Amalie thrashed as three guards grabbed her. "Simon, stop them!"

Beside her, Simon bucked and fought but there were too

many. He went impossibly still as the hilt of a sword struck him in the head.

"Please," she yelled as a hand pushed her to her knees. "Leave them alone."

Anders only glanced at her in pity. "All those associated with the Hood are a threat."

Seconds later, guards dragged Tuck from the chapel unconscious. Ayden wasn't far behind.

"Sara!" he screamed. "Sara!"

Amalie met his defeated gaze, and she tried to jump to her feet and run into the chapel. A hand yanked her back.

"They killed her." Ayden's entire body shook. "My Sara is dead."

The words sank like a stone in Amalie's stomach. Sara, the woman who'd spent the last year keeping Amalie's daughter safe had paid for it with her life.

Amalie ripped her arm free and twisted to kick the man who held her. She tried to draw her sword, but he knocked it from her hand.

"Where's El?" She tried to get to Ayden, but the hard hilt of a sword struck her gut and she fell back. Mud splashed her face, and she wiped it away.

She tore her eyes from Ayden just in time to see a final guard leave the chapel with a little girl draped over his arms. Amalie cried out as a guard yanked her to her feet.

The guard holding El handed her to Anders. "Dead, sir."

"No!" The air left Amalie's lungs, and she gasped for breath. Everything crumbled around her until she no longer recognized where she was. Every part of her ached. She'd failed.

When a guard lifted her off the ground, she no longer fought. When he put chains on her wrists, she held them still for him. As they loaded her into the back of a wagon, all she wanted to do was join her sweet girl in peaceful slumber.

Chapter

Twenty-Five

"Are you sure this is the right place?" Tyson scanned the small cellar below the derelict chapel.

John's troubled eyes traveled the dirt floor before something caught his attention. He reached toward Edmund and grabbed the torch from him before crossing the small space and crouching low.

Tyson followed him. "What is it? What do you see?"

John looked up, meeting Tyson's eyes. "Blood." His brow creased. "Fresh blood."

"They were here." Tyson didn't know whether to feel relieved or alarmed. They'd traveled days to the village but seen no sign of Amalie other than a camp in the woods where a few men corralled horses. They hadn't approached it, not wanting to be delayed.

Edmund blew out a breath. "Well, that's better than what we had before." They'd first gone to the house John claimed was where Amalie would have gone, but it was swarming with soldiers.

Tyson rubbed the back of his neck. "That depends on whose blood this is. They wouldn't kill her, would they? She's still a noble lady of Gaule. My mother wouldn't stand for it. She loves Amalie."

John straightened. "She did. Once. But there have been years of strife between the queen and those on the Leroy lands."

Tyson hardened his jaw and repeated his words. "My mother wouldn't kill her." She knew it would destroy her son, but that wasn't the true reason. There'd been a time when Amalie was like a daughter to the queen. When she'd lived in the palace after they convicted her father of treason. Those times seemed like a distant past from a far-off land.

Edmund pulled Tyson away from John and lowered his voice. "You forget who has been searching for her. Amalie is a known friend of magic folk and my father hates us most of all. He'll have no mercy for her. Her crimes only give him the excuse he needs to make an example. Especially here on the border where the battle with magic has caused much strife. Your mother would stop this were she here, but my father has always preferred asking forgiveness rather than permission."

Captain Anders had long been a problem officer in Gaule. There was a time Tyson thought he'd be banished for disobeying the crown. But Anders always managed the wriggle out of whatever situation he put himself in.

Still, he knew Amalie.

John's voice intruded on their private conversation. "The Captain has been searching for the Hood since she began his mission. It's an obsession for him. Many of his men have died while trying to find her and the rumor is the queen has lost confidence in him for his lack of results. He's lost everything. He'll want to make a spectacle of this, no doubt."

Tyson's fists clenched at his sides as he thought of what

Amalie must be going through. Why had she come here? Willingly walking into a trap. "That means we still have time."

John nodded. "Exactly."

Tyson walked toward the stairs. "We'll find them. Edmund, I need you to go back to the camp in the woods. If anyone got away, they'll return there for supplies. I need any information you can gather."

Edmund didn't argue. "Where will you be?"

Tyson glanced at John. He didn't trust the man and wouldn't let him out of his sight, but he also needed him. "We'll go to the house where it seems like the royal guard has set up post. We can monitor their movements. Eventually, they'll lead us to where we need to be."

Edmund grabbed his arm. "I will return to you at dawn."

Tyson placed his hand over Edmund's. "Be careful."

"You too, Ty." He hesitated. "I know how much you love her... but don't play the hero. Don't sacrifice yourself."

"Edmund, when Stev was a prisoner in Madra, did you worry about your own safety? When you almost died for him, did you think your sacrifice was worth it? Would you have given everything you had to break him free?"

Edmund released him, but didn't step away. "I hope she deserves you, Ty."

Even after everything she'd done, that didn't seem to matter anymore. Amalie tried to break him, yet it changed nothing. "I love her, Edmund. I've spent most of my life loving her. That isn't something she has earned or something she can lose. It just is. There's no stopping it. It's like my magic, a force inside my soul that I have little control over." He gave Edmund a sad smile. "Be safe, my friend."

Stepping past his greatest friend, he considered his own words. Over the years, he'd tried to gain some level of control over his feelings for Amalie, lessen it somehow. Sometimes he didn't want to feel anything at all.

But he was wrong. When he'd let her push him away. When he'd thought she was lost to him. And again, when he left only days ago, planning to never return. His entire life, he'd had people around him to show him what it was to be cared for, to know someone would always come to save him.

It was time to show Amalie what she'd never known. She was not alone. She never had been.

John followed him from the chapel into the half-deserted town. Many of the buildings were still fire scorched and crumbling from the battles years before. Some of the residents had retreated to Bela and others had fled into the interior of Gaule in fear of La Dame. Many never returned.

Neither man spoke for a long while until John's voice filled the space between them. "I didn't know."

Tyson didn't look at him. "There are a lot of things you didn't know."

"The things you said to Edmund..." He sucked in a breath as if the words hurt to say. "I hated you. When I was a prisoner and then after Amalie set me free. You had everything. You were a prince of two kingdoms and Amalie loved you. Your life seemed easy compared to that of a beggar boy who had to scrounge for every scrap he received."

"You know nothing about me or my life," Tyson growled. "I had to run from the palace when my own brother was king because having magic once meant death in this kingdom. The person who was supposed to get me out—who I later learned was my sister—was arrested and imprisoned. Then, La Dame took me. I spent weeks as her prisoner, doing her bidding while my brother was locked in her tower. I fought a war, thinking none of us would survive it, so La Dame didn't take control of

Gaule and Bela, so people like you didn't become prey to her whims."

He kicked at a rock on the ground, the toe of his boot sticking in mud. "Easy." He scoffed. "There is nothing easy in this life, John Little. The people in the villages don't own hardship or strife. But you don't get that. Neither does Amalie. Gaule is falling apart, yet she thinks only those she wishes to serve have troubles. What about the men she sticks her arrows in? Or the queen who lost the father of her child to an outlaw?"

"Simon?" John's jaw fell open.

Tyson didn't answer him. He turned the corner onto another empty street. Those who lived in this part of town were safe in their beds with no idea of what happened in their village that night.

Tyson, John, and Edmund had left their horses behind, choosing to venture into the village on foot to draw less attention. The guards had known Amalie was coming, but Tyson had the benefit of surprise.

They took the better part of an hour to reach the seemingly sleepy house. It backed up to a courtyard shared by four other houses. A man in a simple tunic and brown trousers sat in a chair out front, his eyes closed as if asleep.

But Tyson knew better. "One guard on the porch," he said. "Where are the others?"

John pressed himself into the shadows across the street. "They already have Amalie. They think no one will come for her."

"Do you think she's in there?"

"It doesn't matter."

Tyson snapped his eyes to John. "What do you mean it doesn't matter?"

"We can't go in there for her. We'll have to wait until they bring her out."

Tyson's shoulders dropped, and he rubbed a hand across his face. John was right, and Tyson couldn't use his magic to get in without risking everyone inside the building.

He jerked his head toward a building nearby with broken windows. "Abandoned?"

John pushed away from the wall. "Half the homes in this forsaken town are, so good chance." He slammed his foot into the wooden door. It splintered and broke inward. He kicked it again, and it burst open.

Tyson looked inside, waiting for any residents to come out screaming. No one came. He entered, eyes scanning the front room. Broken furniture lay scattered around the space, but nothing else of value sat within view. "Looters."

John shrugged and kicked broken glass from a spot near one of the windows before removing his cloak and laying it on the ground. He sat, his eyes focused on the house nearby. Tyson leaned against the wall. If he sat, he worried his tired body would relax into sleep.

Throughout the night, no guards came or went. Tyson eventually let himself relax onto the floor, and his eyes drifted shut of their own accord.

By the time he woke, a dim light filtered through the window and muffled voices reached his ears. He sat up quickly, all sleep fading from his mind as he caught sight of Edmund talking to John and... Simon? He jumped to his feet and rushed toward them.

"Si, where's Amalie?"

Simon's lips drew down. "They're keeping her locked in a room across the street with her men."

"How did you get out?"

Simon glanced from John to Tyson as if trying to decide what to say. "A few of Captain Anders men used to be mine. They follow him now, but they also know holding me prisoner is no way to gain favor with the crown... They also wanted me to get the child to safety."

"Child?" Tyson finally saw the sleeping form wrapped in a cloak on the floor near Simon's feet.

John crouched down, pushing the cloak back from the girl's face. "Elayne." He said her name in reverence as if not quite believing she was there with them.

Simon addressed John. "Amalie thinks the child is dead."

John lifted his face, pain in his eyes. "That's... They're destroying her."

The girl roused herself, lifting her head of dark hair. Large sapphire eyes landed on Tyson, and something inside him stirred. He couldn't explain it but it was as if his magic called to her.

"Simon." He could barely breathe. "Who is this child?"

Before Simon could respond, the girl wiggled out of the cloak and stood on wobbly legs. She reached out a hand, connecting her skin to Tyson's. Warmth spread through him, a happiness he hadn't felt in years. He could sense it. Her magic. It covered him in a blanket of comfort.

But it was too much, too false. There was no happiness that lived inside him while Amalie marched to her death. He snatched his hand back, and the girl gave him a questioning gaze.

"She has magic." He turned away from them and paced the length of the room. He stopped in front of them once more.

John shook his head. "I didn't know." He put his hands on his head in exasperation. "We should have guessed. She would never be safe in this village with magic in her blood." He leaned against the wall and slid down. "What have we done?" His face fell into his hands. "I told her to do it. That she had to do it to keep the girl safe, to continue on with her mission."

"Told who?" Tyson yelled. "I need to know what's going

on." Suspicion warred in him as he looked at the girl once more. He shook his head and backed away. "She couldn't... she... Amalie?"

"Tyson." Edmund tried to calm him.

Tyson pushed him away and advanced on John. "This is why she came?" It all made so much sense now. "I need you to say it, John. I need to hear the words."

John lifted a tortured face. "Amalie is the girl's mother."

Tyson stumbled back as the words battered into his chest. His eyes fell on the girl they'd called Elayne. She couldn't be much more than a year old, probably less. And her magic... His breath clogged in his throat until he couldn't breathe.

Amalie, how could you do this?

He thought he knew her—that he knew the worst sins of her heart, but he'd been wrong. "John, when Amalie sent for me..."

"It was the childbirth killing her," John finished. "She'd have had you take the girl."

He shook his head. "Get out before I kill you."

John opened his mouth to respond, but Tyson pulled water in from the rain-soaked streets with his power and sent it barreling into John's chest, throwing him through the broken window. John sputtered and picked himself up out in the street. "What about Amalie?"

Tyson's eyes blazed. "We don't need you to save her."

It went against everything Tyson believed in to use his magic to fight every battle. He'd done it before, but never with such premeditated intent. This time, though, Anders would pay.

Tyson's anger lessened until it only simmered inside him as his eyes found Elayne once more. She cowered against Simon's leg. Fear sprang to her eyes when she lifted them to Tyson, and it sent a dagger straight through his heart.

He wiped a hand over his face, regaining his composure. His

magic once again reached out to her, and he dropped to his knees.

"I'm not going to hurt you," he whispered, holding a hand out to her.

She only hesitated a moment before taking it. The warmth of her power mended his frayed nerves.

How had he not seen it immediately? She looked every bit like his mother, the queen. The dark curls. Wide eyes. But there was some Basile in her as well. Tyson thought nothing could make him feel whole again after the hell of the last few years, but as he stared into the face of a girl who was a part of him, he felt some of the cracks in his soul heal themselves.

He knew then that everything Amalie had done was to protect the one person in this world she'd always love. She'd given her up, wanting the child to have no connection to the Hood. She'd come back when the danger reached her daughter's doorstep.

Tyson cupped Elayne's tiny cheek in his palm before pulling her into his chest. Her little body shook in his arms. He couldn't imagine what she'd been through in the last day, but she released it all.

Tears filled his eyes as she asked, "Mama?" It took him a moment to realize she didn't mean Amalie.

Simon smoothed a hand over Elayne's head and whispered to Tyson and Edmund. "Her mother was killed by the guards yesterday. Captain Anders has her father imprisoned with Amalie."

Tyson lifted Elayne into his arms and passed her to Simon, hating to relinquish her safety to anyone else. "Si, you've already done more than we deserve, but I need you to do one more thing for me."

Simon nodded for him to go on.

Tyson breathed deeply before he could force the words out.

"Leave. Take Elayne from this place." He closed his eyes for a moment. "Today, Edmund and I will go against an untold number of guards. I can't do that unless she's safe, and she won't be safe in Gaule. Get her to Bela, to my brother and sister. Please. I can't..."

Edmund put a hand on his shoulder, and Tyson was grateful for the support.

"I can't risk myself unless I know she's safe."

Simon nodded. "I'll protect her as if she was my own."

"You're a good man, Si. There isn't enough time in this life to repay you for everything you've done for me over the years." He leaned forward, pressing his shaking lips to the back of the girl's head.

It wasn't enough time. He'd only had minutes to come to terms with his fatherhood, but nothing had ever felt so important in his life.

And it only strengthened his resolve. He wouldn't leave his child without a mother.

"They're leaving." Edmund fixed his eyes on the house across the street where a line of shackled prisoners streamed out the front door and down the street. They were out of time.

He nodded to Simon once more before grabbing his bow and sword, leaving through the back into an alleyway between homes.

Edmund caught up with him. "We'll save her, Ty. Then they'll both be okay."

He wished he was as confident. "Edmund, we have to use our magic."

Edmund didn't respond.

"It's Amalie. I know how you feel about using it in Gaule, and it probably means we're going to have to run from this place with a mob demanding our deaths, but—"

"Ty." Edmund gripped his shoulder, pulling him to a stop. "If there's ever a time to fight using whatever we have, this is it."

Tyson breathed out in relief. They wound through back alleys and side streets, trying not to lose sight of the prisoner train. Guards lined the street, more than Tyson could count in a hurry.

"I don't like this," Edmund whispered.

Tyson didn't stop moving.

Edmund spoke again. "Ty, my father—"

"Needs to be stopped."

"I know that better than anyone." Edmund cursed as his foot hit a water-filled hole in the road and he stumbled forward. Righting himself, he grunted. "But there are a lot of soldiers we have to go through. Your mother's soldiers."

"My mother would never stand for this, for her guard to be used in such a way."

Edmund stepped in front of him and turned. "Ty, if we're going to do this, you need to go in with open eyes. The queen might not allow Amalie to be treated this way. She'd do everything to save her granddaughter, but she has also allowed her guard to rove the land in search of outlaws. Amalie is the person they think she is. She is the Hood. But many who've been captured before her were innocent. They. Do. Not. Care. We aren't just going to grab Amalie and escape. We'll need to fight."

"I know that."

"Do you?" His eyes burned into Tyson. "After we do this, that's it. You will no longer be able to set foot in Gaule. Your old home will be lost to you. You won't see your mother unless she makes royal visits to Bela. Royal visits that may cease after this. After two Belaens use their magic against an entire unit of the royal guard. This is the end of your life as a prince of two kingdoms. After this, you will only have one."

Tyson lifted his chin. "And you don't think every word

you've said hasn't occurred to me? You don't think it's worth it to me? Like I said, I know what this will cost. And just like those guards, I do not care."

A grim smile spread across Edmund's face. "Then we fight. I never wanted to return to Gaule, anyway. Exile will be a welcome fate."

"And your father? Can you truly fight him?"

Edmund turned and started walking again. "That man is no father of mine."

"Thank you. For doing this for me."

Edmund shrugged. "It's what we do. We come for each other. No matter which of the six kingdoms tries to strike us down, we aren't alone in our fights. Ever."

Tyson thought of the little girl he'd sent with Simon. Elayne. And her mother. They weren't alone either. They had him.

Chapter

Twenty-Six

Ayden was dead. He'd tried to escape in the night only to receive a sword through the belly. He'd left the world behind. Just like his wife and daughter. Daughter. Amalie closed her eyes picturing rosy cheeks and a kind smile. Yes, she was Ayden and Sara's. Amalie had no claim over the mother's grief raging through her. She'd given her up. No matter the reason, however noble the cause, it didn't change the facts.

Amalie no longer cared what waited for her at the end of the long walk. She was finished, done with a life of hiding. Through with the pain of losing everything she loved again and again.

If this was brokenness, she hoped the cracks shattered her completely.

Behind her, Tuck whispered soft prayers to himself. He didn't deserve what was coming. He hadn't deserved to watch them carry his sister's limp body from the cellar below the chapel where he'd once performed weddings. How could such a happy place be stained with so much blood and so many tears?

In front of her, the men and women who'd placed their faith in the Hood walked to their ends. Thieving was punishable by death as was abduction and attacking royal forces. All of which they were guilty of.

But they were good, trying to make some sense of their shit world by helping those who couldn't help themselves. They'd given up everything to join her, to become her Merry Men. And it seemed they'd make one final sacrifice.

Will lumbered at her side, a hulking mercenary who'd once killed for gold. Far off in the distance lay the walls of Dracon, a kingdom once ruled by the dark sorceress, La Dame. A kingdom Will had fought for, bled for. He'd joined the Hood out of some misguided notion of atonement. Would this final act absolve him of his sins?

The town's scaffolds came into view as the guards marched them into the square. Villagers mingled nearby, waiting to witness the act, relieved that this time, it wasn't them waiting for the ground to fall underneath their feet.

Amalie wanted to hate them, but she couldn't muster a shred of emotion.

Everything was a calculated move by Captain Anders. He'd announce the names of the prisoners before ushering them into their final moments. The news of the Hood's demise would spread throughout the kingdom and his fame would only grow. The people would fear him. They'd obey him.

The queen would be distraught upon hearing the news, but would she be more upset that her precious Amalie had deceived her or that she'd been hung with no trial, no chance for absolution.

The guards had learned their lesson with John's execution. No friar stood waiting to give last rites. They cleared each surrounding building, allowing nowhere safe for a rescuer to hide.

What they didn't understand was there was no one left to rescue her. Everyone who may have tried was either a prisoner or far away in another kingdom.

Tyson would hear of her death eventually, but he'd never know the secrets she took with her. He'd never learn how she'd deceived him and kept him from looking in to the face of their daughter, born of a love so intense it haunted her days and filled her nights with never-ending darkness.

Amalie lifted her face to the morning sun. The gray skies of the day before had disappeared, leaving a dazzling blue in their wake. At least she wouldn't spend her final day in shadow.

She scanned the backs of each man in front of her, making a mental note of the names of those crossing over with her. They deserved to be remembered even if she wasn't there to shout their names.

One was missing, but she wasn't surprised. Anders couldn't punish Simon, the queen's own man. Just like the others, he'd tied himself to the Hood when he journeyed to the border village with her. Where had he gone?

She scanned the surrounding area. Maybe he couldn't watch. She didn't blame him for staying away.

Tuck sucked in a breath behind her. She turned her head. "What is it?"

"Oy!" a red-headed guard to their right yelled. "Shut yer mouth." He moved past them.

Tuck leaned in, his breath blowing across her cheek. "John is here."

She searched the crowd, finding him quickly. He had a scarf wrapped around the lower half of his face, but she'd recognize those eyes anywhere.

"I don't know what he thinks he can do against all these guards." She lifted her hand to brush it through her hair but the iron chains stopped it halfway there.

"Ames..."

She shook her head, stepping away from Tuck. There were no more words to be said. Accepting defeat was one of the tenants of a great warrior. She'd had years of glory, saved many people. It was someone else's turn now.

She rubbed a sore spot, remembering the sword hilt that had rammed into her when she tried to get to El's body. They hadn't let her see her or say goodbye. One of the guards had walked past Amalie's temporary cell carrying a still bundle in his arms. He hadn't even glanced at her.

Amalie thought the safest place for El would be in a rural town living as an unremarkable girl. She was wrong. She should have known they'd get to her eventually. That the Hood's enemies were relentless and ruthless. Finding the child was the one surefire way to draw Amalie into their trap.

Now she was a prisoner, and it had all been for nothing because she couldn't save her. Elayne was dead. The light she'd been in the world was extinguished, leaving only ash behind.

Her eyes found John once more on the edge of the crowd. He'd done so much wrong, but the Hood wouldn't have existed without him. Even after the tragic end of her mission, she couldn't regret it. She wouldn't take it back. For a short time, she'd had purpose. There was a reason she was still there when everyone else who bore the Leroy name was gone.

For a while, she'd bested them. Her father, a traitor just as she was, did not control how she would be remembered. From this day forward, Amalie Leroy would not be spoken of in hushed tones as people cursed her father.

No, she'd be known as the woman who inspired her people in a way even the queen could not. She lifted her chin. She wasn't a fire to be stamped out by the boot of the crown.

She was an uncontrollable blaze at the edge of the kingdom,

catching fire to everything she touched. Gaule couldn't go back. They couldn't forget.

A guard grabbed her arm, jerking her forward. She stumbled until she stood at the edge of the raised platform. The wood hit her mid-chest, digging into her flesh as she knew the swinging rope soon would.

The guards pushed two of her men up the steps to where their end waited. A masked figure stood at the lever, his dark eyes catching hers. A hand landed on her back, pushing her forward. The crowd murmured words she couldn't make out. Were they shocked to see a woman preparing to hang? Did they care?

She sucked in a breath. They would.

Her feet took the four steps slowly, deliberately. Her eyes didn't leave the crowd. They wouldn't escape the memory of her fiery gaze. Three nooses hung in a row. Once her legs stopped kicking and her lungs stopped expanding, the executioners would move on as if she hadn't been there at all. Those behind her in line would suffer more for having to watch their comrades lose their final battle before hanging themselves.

She no longer cared what happened to her, but her people deserved better.

Hands gripped her shoulders, moving her toward the farthest rope. Will stood beside her, loyal to the end. He issued a prayer to the heavens. On his other side, one of her most loyal guards, Cam, stood stoically.

The heavy stomp of Anders' boots alerted them to his presence behind them as he climbed onto the platform and addressed the crowd.

"This is a good day in Gaule," he began. "A good day indeed. You may have noticed the royal guard overrunning your village for the past two days. The queen sent us on a mission to capture the most notorious traitor in the kingdom." He paused.

"The Hood." The crowd gasped. Eyes bounced from Cam to Will as they tried to discern which man was the outlaw they'd heard so much about.

Anders went on. "The Hood is no symbol of hope as you've been led to believe." He turned his gaze on Amalie. "She is nothing more than a thief."

Someone in the crowd screamed while others clamored for answers.

"The Hood is a woman?"

"She fights for us."

"Free her."

"She betrayed our queen."

All these sentiments and more swirled in the air, but Amalie paid them no mind. Her only focus was on Anders, the man who'd taken everything from her when his men killed El. If her hands weren't chained behind her back, she'd wrap them around his neck and squeeze the life from his bones.

He raised a brow as if he could hear her dark thoughts before turning back to the crowd. "The Hood steals at her pleasure. She murders the innocent and abducts those with the ear of the queen." He let his words settle over them. "She harbors magic folk."

Their gasps were all Amalie needed to know the captain had won the people to his side. Magic was no longer illegal in Gaule, but in the small villages, especially those along the border who'd been harmed the most, magic meant evil. Their irrational hatred of it blinded them to all else.

One of the guards hauled Maiya forward. "A Draconian in the Hood's employ." The air changed and those who'd voice their support for Amalie only moments ago, yelled demands for her end.

These people hated all those with magic, but Draconians

inspired a special kind of ire. They'd once belonged to La Dame. Maiya herself had been the sorceress' slave.

But they didn't understand what Amalie always had. Everyone had evil inside them. She lowered her gaze to John who'd moved closer. The difference between good and bad lay in the decision to let that evil out.

A guard slid the noose over Amalie's head. The rope bit into her skin as he tightened it, sliding the knot until it lay underneath her chin.

A calm overcame her, and she closed her eyes, ignoring the rest of Captain Anders' words.

When it came time for the accused to make their final confessions, Cam was first. He lifted his voice. "I have no confession to make. I have lived my life in good conscience and regret nothing. You people want blood? Look to those who've held you down. The Hood only ever tried to lift the common man up. You should be ashamed of yourselves. You think this is the queen's desire? She will not stand for this."

He swept his eyes over the crowd before meeting Amalie's gaze one final time. Cam had been one of her father's men, but through no choice of his own. He'd been the first to switch his allegiance to her and stayed at her side since.

He deserved better than an angry mob and a noose. For the first time that day, a tear slipped down her cheek. He gave his head a tiny shake and opened his mouth to speak one final time. Whatever he'd wanted to say was cut off as the floor beneath him dropped open and the sickening snap of bone ripped through the air.

He didn't move as he hung there. There was no more struggle left in him. The crowd let a few moments pass in impossible silence before the horror struck them. Amalie forced a breath out past her lips, her fate feeling real for the first time.

She pictured Cam marching through her estate on the day

he pledged his allegiance to her. She'd thrown most of her father's men from her home as soon as she took it back from the queen. But he'd been so sincere, so true. And she'd never regretted the trust she placed in him. He'd been one of the first in her band of Hood followers.

Anders looked to Will. "Speak."

Will's jaw clenched, and he fixed his eyes on the distance, not looking at the crowd, refusing to utter a single word.

"I'm sorry," Amalie whispered. She'd led them here. She'd killed them all.

Will finally turned his head to her, his words so low only she could hear. "I've done so much wrong in my life. I never thought I'd get to die for something good."

Will had come to her a year after the Draconian war. He'd chosen not to remain with the mercenaries who fought for the dark sorceress, leaving him alone and hungry. He'd attacked her camp, but left her unharmed. She didn't know what she'd seen in him that day. A need for redemption? Desperation. Her men searched until they found him. The day he finally pledged loyalty to her, she realized anyone could be saved. Anyone could be good if they desired it. That knowledge shaped the Hood into who she became.

When the door underneath Will's feet opened, a scream lodged in her throat. She cried not for herself, but for everyone who'd followed her so blindly to this fate. Tears rolled down her cheeks unchecked, proving to her in her final moments that her heart still beat inside her chest. That she could still feel something after she thought the cold would never cease.

Fire raged in her belly as she lifted her eyes to Anders. "You think this is the end." She raised her voice so others could hear, but her focus remained on the captain. "But my mission will never end. The people deserve more than they're given. Someone will give it to them. Someone will replace me. We are not disposable." She stilled her quivering lips. "This was never about me. The Hood never belonged to me. This kingdom is falling apart village by village. Soon, it will tumble so far into the abyss, not even Catrine can pull it back. Your hatred has blinded you."

She looked to where a guard still held Maiya by the arm. "Her magic heals people while your hatred of it tears them apart." She lifted her eyes to the brilliant blue above. "I am ready to die, but my mission is woven into the fabric of this kingdom. I do not take it with me."

She closed her eyes, listening to the gears underneath her feet as they worked to open the hole that would take her to another world.

For a moment, she suspended in air before her body dropped and the rope inched up, cutting off the last breath she hadn't had time to take.

Chapter

Twenty-Seven

Tyson pushed through the crowded alleyway. Everyone in the village had come, clogging the streets. Guards lined the rooftops overlooking the square. And he had no way to get to the platform.

He rammed his shoulder into a couple in front of him, breaking them apart and darting through the gap they created. He'd lost Edmund, but they both knew what they had to do.

A gasp reverberated around the crowd as Anders' voice rose above them all, revealing the Hood for who she was. Tyson couldn't hear the rest of the Captain's words over the din of the surrounding people.

He stumbled as he knocked into a large man. His hands slammed into the stone walkway and he scrambled back to his feet, lifting his eyes to the platform.

Amalie stood next to Will and Cam, her eyes closed. Was she afraid? Did she feel the same fear that sliced through Tyson's heart?

His magic pooled in his fingertips, but he couldn't release it yet. They had a plan. Saving Amalie from the hangman's noose was only the beginning. They also had to escape the village.

He scanned the lines of guards in the eaves. They pointed arrows toward the crowd as if expecting an incursion.

A guard bulled through the crowd, towing Maiya behind him. He shoved her forward, proof that the Hood wasn't someone the villagers should want to follow. They'd carry the knowledge of her acceptance of magic far and wide.

She'd go from revered hero to scorned traitor. It no longer mattered in Gaule what the crown's view on magic was. They didn't care whether it was legal or not.

The people would always fear the power. They'd always hate the ones who wielded it. Anger sizzled along Tyson's skin as the crowd turned on Amalie, calling for her death. If they hated magic so much, he'd give them true reason to fear it.

He'd show them what it could truly do.

He made his way to the line of shops across the square and searched the empty buildings until he found a bucket of wash water sitting behind a counter. As he carried it outside, a guard stopped him.

"Oy, no one is allowed inside during the demonstration."

Demonstration? That was what they were calling executions now? He tamped down his ire and smiled nervously. "I'm sorry, sir." He pointed to a horse he'd never seen before. "My beast there needs a wee drink." He held up the pail with a shrug.

The guard considered him for a moment before gesturing for him to leave. Tyson walked toward the horse until the guard no longer watched him and then veered away.

He'd only turned his back for a moment when a thump sounded behind him. He whipped his head around to find Cam's swinging from a rope. They were too late. His neck must have broken because his legs didn't thrash. His face changed color as his head lulled forward.

They were out of time.

Tyson's gaze scanned the surroundings, searching for Edmund. Why hadn't he been in position yet? Another crash broke through the chaos of Tyson's mind.

Will.

He shook his head, alarm raising the hair on his arms. He needed Edmund. If he tried to use his water magic to save Amalie, he'd just as likely drown her or weaken himself into a state that did neither of them any good.

"Where are you, Edmund?"

He was so focused on finding Edmund, he didn't hear most of Amalie's words until one phrase stuck in his mind. "I'm ready to die."

No. He wasn't ready for her to die. He shouldered through the crowd, ignoring the nasty looks directed his way as water sloshed over the sides of the pail. He was only steps away when the door beneath Amalie's feet crashed open. Her body jerked as it fell through the gap.

Tyson screamed, the sound enveloping him in a haze of panic. He dropped the bucket to the ground and drew the water towards him, his power attaching to every drop. The magic flowed through him like a rushing river wanting to break free of the dam.

Anger fueled it. Desperation made it uncontrollable. Grief turned it deadly.

The water expanded in the air before contracting to form a solid wall. He pushed it out from himself and it exploded forth, striking the guards and villagers nearest, sending them crashing to the ground, unconscious. He pulled it back just enough to prevent them from drowning.

Wave after wave of magic released from his every pore. No

one was safe. Royal guards. Innocent villagers. Men. Women. Children.

Prisoner or free.

They all experienced what true power meant. What it could do to them. Tyson twisted his body, sending the water spiraling, a cyclone smashing through the crowd as they screamed and ran, seeking any kind of safety.

Tyson's chest heaved with the effort and he stumbled back, the magic pulling every bit of energy from his limbs.

He lifted his head, seeing Captain Anders trying to pick himself up off the ground. He'd been knocked from the platform. Tyson clung to every bit of strength he had left as he advanced.

The first true fear he'd ever seen in Anders crossed his face. Tyson had known the Captain since he was a child. He'd been a loyal follower of the man Tyson once thought was his father. He'd caused trouble since that king died, betraying Alex and taking advantage of his mother now that she was queen. He had to be stopped.

He only gave small thought to the knowledge that this was Edmund's father. The fact remained. He'd killed Amalie. He'd taken everything from Tyson.

Tyson let the magic take control, burning along his skin. He drew water from the ground, letting it pool at his feet.

"My prince." Anders stumbled back. "Please. I am your mother's man."

Tyson growled at that. "Do not mention my mother to me. If she knew what you were truly doing..." He shook his head. "No, you don't get to plead for your life." His eyes darkened as he thought of the final moments of life the three now hanging had. "Consider these your last rites. Confess your sins, Captain."

Anders shook his head, his gaze searching the ground.

Tyson sent a spear of water to wash away the knife that lay near his feet. His impatience grew, but Anders remained silent.

I'm ready to die. Amalie's words rang in his ears. Anders did that to her. He took her desire to live. Tyson curled his fingers, pressing them into his palms as his pulse hammered in his head.

Captain Anders considered him dangerous, not a true prince because of his Belaen heritage, because of his magic. He didn't know the half of it.

Tyson flicked one palm open, sending a torrent of water flooding into Anders' every orifice. It streamed through his mouth. His nose. His ears. Taking everything from him, emptying him. The water roared like a rushing river, never wanting to stop as it pulled the life from the man who'd hurt so many people.

Until finally, the captain crumpled right where he stood.

Tyson fell to his knees, tears streaming down his face. He cried for Amalie. For all the death he'd seen and caused. He could feel his soul shattering. Tyson had killed people before, but only in war.

He supposed this was a kind of war.

Around him, villagers picked themselves up off the ground. Guards tried to contain the mass confusion. The other prisoners remained chained together.

Tyson fell forward onto his hands, struggling to keep his eyes open. It took everything he had to lift his head for one final glance at where Amalie hung lifeless.

Only, what he saw returned some bit of the strength he'd lost.

Amalie hovered, noose still around her neck but not pulled taught. A tunnel of wind kept her from dropping. Her wide eyes found him.

He pushed himself off the ground, stumbling to his feet as he ran on uncoordinated legs. Someone else reached her before him, jumping onto the platform, knife in hand. John's scarf fell, revealing his haggard face. He held a knife in his teeth as he reached for the rope. He grabbed it and sawed through the fraying threads. The rope dropped over Amalie's shoulder and the wind lessened, lowering her to the ground.

Tyson lunged forward to catch her before her legs collapsed beneath her. They fell to the ground, both too weak to hold the other up.

"Ty?" she whispered, tears springing to her eyes.

Tyson pressed his forehead to hers. "I'm here, Ames. I'm here." Her entire body shook as Tyson rocked her in his arms.

Edmund stumbled out from where he'd hidden himself in an empty storefront. "I was too late." He fixed his eyes on Cam and Will. "I'm sorry."

She didn't respond as she clung to Tyson.

Tyson had almost forgotten about the guards still in the village. He had no more strength to fight as they closed in around them. It wasn't over yet.

"Magic man," one of the guards shouted. Not prince or highness. If they addressed him with the respect his birth earned him, they'd have to face what they did.

His eyes slid shut as he waited for them to issue their final condemnation. The few villagers who hadn't fled for their lives, now stood soaking from head to toe. They screamed and jeered, calling for Tyson's head.

They'd known of their prince's magic before, but now that he'd used it against them, he was no longer one of them.

Finally, he lifted his head to look at the guard. "What do you want from me?"

The guard strode forward a few steps before veering to the right and stopping in front of Edmund. "You are under arrest for your attack on Gaule."

Tyson tried to untangle himself from Amalie and push

himself to his feet. His mother's men couldn't arrest Tyson without raising questions from the queen, but Edmund was different.

Tyson tried to call on his magic, but all strength had left him. Edmund's entire body sagged with weakness, but he held his chin high and drew his sword. "You can try." His sword wavered as he struggled to hold it up. His magic had depleted him.

The guard lunged forward as Edmund's sword dipped low. Tyson didn't have time to scream a warning before someone rammed into Edmund's side, throwing him out of the way. The guard's sword bit into flesh.

Edmund hit the ground hard, his sword skittering away. But that wasn't the sight that had them all gaping in horror.

The guard slid his bloodstained blade free of John's side. John looked down in shock and lifted a hand to feel for the wound. Blood seeped through his fingers as he faltered back, his stance wavering. "Amalie, I'm sorry." His eyes met Amalie's as he sank to his knees.

Chapter

Twenty-Eight

Amalie choked on a breath as she forced her body to move, pushing away from Tyson. John. She had to get to John.

The guard stood over him, a scowl on his face. "Traitors always get what they deserve."

Amalie knew the words were meant for her, but at that moment, she didn't care. All she saw was her oldest friend lying in the dirt with his life seeping out of him. For her. It was all for her.

She reached his side, and the guard didn't stop her as she rolled John onto his back. His breath rasped out as if liquid filled his lungs.

It no longer mattered what he'd done to her. She didn't see the man who'd kept Tyson from her these last few years or the one who'd lied countless times. She'd worried for so long about the blood he'd spilled, not knowing what kind of man that made him. But now, as he tried to speak, the only blood staining his hands was his own. He was still the boy she'd known. The one who'd convinced her she could make a difference, that she wasn't tainted by the name of her family.

"John." His name was only a whisper on her lips, but he snapped his eyes to hers.

"Ames." His chest shook as he coughed.

"Shhhh." She brushed the sopping hair from his forehead. He'd been hit with Tyson's magic, yet he still saved Edmund. For the past couple years, he'd spoken of how magic had no place in Gaule. And yet in his final moment, he'd given himself up for it.

"That's enough." The guard gripped Amalie's arm and yanked her to her feet.

"No." She tried to fight him, but he was too strong. "John!"

"Ames." Tears streamed down John's cheeks. "Ames, I'm sorry." His eyes slid closed.

"No! Don't you die on me, John Little." She slammed her head back until it connected with the guard's nose. He released her with a curse, and she ran back to John's side. "They've taken everything from me, John. You can't do this. It's supposed to be you and me against the world."

He didn't respond. Amalie shook her head, rage thrumming through her. An arm wrapped around her waist, pulling her back, but she wasn't the grieving damsel they thought she was.

She was the Hood.

And the Hood took care of her people.

Amalie slammed her foot back, catching the guard in the knee. She clutched her hands together and brought them down on his hands as hard as she could, breaking his grasp and giving her the opening she needed.

She ran past John's now lifeless body to where Tuck and Maiya were still chained with the others. Picking up speed, she rammed into one of the guards hovering near them keeping watch. He stumbled back but didn't fall. By the time he reached for her, she'd knocked the bow from his hands.

Tuck found an arrow one of the guards shot at them during the chaos of magic and threw it to her. She didn't stop running as she set it against the string, feeling more like herself than she had in a long time.

She drew the string and jumped, twisting her body to fire toward her target. The guard who'd killed John clutched at his throat as an arrow pierced his skin. Blood gurgled from his lips as he collapsed next to John.

Amalie landed nimbly on her feet and tossed the bow aside. It was useless to her without more arrows. She bent over the dead guard and lifted his sword, still coated with John's blood. Crimson drops dripped from the tip as she held it in front of herself and faced the remaining guards.

"I know what you've heard about me. The outlaw. The Hood. I'm uncaring. A thief. Unhinged. I kill queen's men just for the pure pleasure of hearing them scream. I'm a traitor from a long line of traitors. Any of this sound familiar?"

She turned in a half circle, meeting each guard's eyes. They didn't approach, but they held their swords ready.

"I wasn't the person you all thought I was. I never betrayed Gaule. I only wanted to save it." She narrowed her eyes. "But now? Unhinged is only the beginning. Before, I had something to protect. My identity. My daughter. But you've ripped the hood from my head. You've taken everything from me." She swept her gaze across the square. "My father used to say the most dangerous person was one with nothing left to lose." She'd lived her life trying to escape her father's legacy. He was an evil man, but he was right in one thing.

Fear was the greatest motivator there was. He'd used the kingdom's fear of magic against the magic-loving king.

The royal guard hadn't chased the Hood for months only because she was a normal thief. They feared her.

She lifted her chin. "Are you going to arrest me?"

As the first guard approached, she focused on the memory of the burn of a rope as it tightened around her neck. When she turned on her heel, launching her knife at the guard, all she saw was Captain Anders offering to let her confess her sins.

As blood sprayed her face, she felt the rush of air as the door opened beneath her feet.

She was ready to die before, but now, she'd take some of the bastards with her.

She didn't notice when Tyson joined in the fight. His movements were slow as he tried to regain his strength. But he was there.

"Tyson, stop," she yelled as she ducked a guard's blade. "This isn't your fight."

She'd gone into this day knowing it would be her last, but Tyson shouldn't have to suffer for her pain.

His sword crashed into his attackers, and he grunted from the effort. "You were wrong, Amalie." He kicked his foot out, catching the guard in the stomach and forcing him back. "They didn't take everything from you."

She grit her teeth as a knife slid across her arm. The physical pain couldn't compare to the agony raging inside her.

"You don't understand, Ty." The guards who jumped into the fight didn't stop. They attacked their prince and the outlaw as if they were ordinary insurgents. Catrine would never stand for this, but she didn't have true control of her kingdom. She wasn't there.

Others hung back, indecision holding them in place. They didn't want to fight the queen's son.

Tyson blocked another attack. "Yes. I do." He let out a roar and jabbed his sword into the man's stomach.

The guard fell off the sword, landing in a heap on the ground.

"I'm not talking about me when I say they haven't taken everything." He readied his stance for another attack. "Elayne. She's alive."

Amalie's sword almost fell out of her grasp. She couldn't have heard his words right. She'd seen El's body, mourned her loss.

Shouting erupted around them, jerking her from her thoughts, as Tuck and the rest of her people joined them. Edmund followed behind, keys still clutched in his grasp. He must have taken them from his father.

Before the guard in front of her could attack, a large hand ripped him back, throwing him farther than any normal man could.

A shudder ran through Amalie as Simon appeared among the guards, the people he should be loyal to. He was a queen's man just as they were. The difference was Simon's true loyalty was to the queen and not the officers.

"Stop this." His voice echoed along the village center. He turned to face the guards. "You would attack your own prince?"

"He's chosen his side," a guard spat.

Simon's movements were so quick, Amalie almost missed them. He flipped a knife into his hand and threw it to the guard who'd spoken. The guard didn't have time to say another word as the knife lodged in the side of his head.

Simon bulled his way back through the crowd to where a village woman stood holding a young girl. He took Elayne into his arms and rejoined the rest, holding her up for them to see. "Do you know who this child is that you tried to murder?"

When no one answered, he shook his head. "She is the queen's own grandchild. Her Majesty will have each of you imprisoned." He set El down. "Unless... stand down. There need be no more fighting this day. Your captain is dead. All blame for this..." His eyes scanned the courtyard. "... event lies with him. If you do not leave this place, there will be consequences. You are no longer welcome among the queen's guards. Whatever you do from here on out will not taint the power of the crown."

Amalie's chest heaved as exhaustion seeped into her. Simon's words stuck in her mind, but all she saw was the child who clung to his leg.

The daughter who did not know her had lost much this day. Both her adopted parents now existed only in the next life.

She'd been ripped from her home and exposed to things no child should have to see.

Tuck appeared at Amalie's side, and she leaned into him as they waited for the guards to make a decision.

Finally, after many long moments, they dispersed, leaving as if they'd never been there at all. But Amalie would never forget and that village would never be the same. Once blood ran in the streets, it was impossible for them to ever truly recover.

Amalie didn't hesitate in running to El and dropping to her knees in front of the girl. Tears clogged in her throat, and she crushed El to her chest. "I'm sorry, my girl. I'm so so sorry."

"Mama?" El's shy voice only deepened the rift within Amalie.

Amalie had rarely been in El's presence, yet she knew every inch of her. And El didn't know Amalie at all. She'd only ever known Sara and Aydan as her parents.

Tyson approached cautiously and set his weapons on the ground. He fell to his knees beside Amalie, and for the first time in a long time, Amalie wanted him there.

She wanted him to look into the face of the best thing either of them had ever done. Tyson slid his hand into Amalie's.

"Elayne." He cupped her cheek with his free hand, leaving a smear of blood on her pale skin.

Amalie ripped Tyson back. They couldn't taint her with their battles. Battles that would never end as long as they remained in Gaule.

She'd once thought nothing could take her from her mission, not even if her identity were discovered. She'd been wrong.

Elayne reached a hand out and laid it on Amalie's shoulder. Warmth spread through her. A kind of happiness she hadn't experienced in years. Her eyes widened. She'd suspected, but hoped it wasn't true. El had magic... just like her father. Those with magic suffered a lot in Gaule.

"Tyson," Amalie whispered. "We have to get her out of here." She looked sideways at him, speaking the words she never thought she'd say. "We need to leave Gaule."

Tyson lifted his eyes to the people trying to put themselves back together. Edmund. Tuck. Maiya. The other loyal people who'd come with them from the Leroy lands. "We all do." He met her gaze. "None of us are safe here anymore."

Edmund approached. "After today, Ty, you and I won't be welcome in Gaule again. Not even your mother can change that."

Tyson flicked his eyes from Amalie to Elayne. "I know. It's time we leave it all behind us."

Amalie stood and lifted El into her arms. The girl curled into her, seeking comfort or warmth. Possibly both. Amalie carried her to where Tuck stood watching Maiya heal the last remaining wounded.

"I'm sorry about your sister. More than you can ever know."

Tuck shook his head, a sad glint in his eye. "She knew the risk she took on by taking El into her home. This wasn't your fault, Ames." He wrapped an arm around her shoulders. "We'll all heal. It'll only take time."

She rested her chin on El's soft curls. "But not here. Not in Gaule."

He brushed a hand over her head. "There's nothing left for me in Gaule. You're my family, Amalie. I'll go wherever you lead."

The weight of the past few days crushed down on her until she could barely stand. Tuck took El from her arms moments before her knees hit the dirt. She covered her face in her hands, but no more tears came. She'd cried every last one she could cry.

Now was a time to be strong, to march into the future, but all Amalie wanted to do was curl up right there on the ground and let her mind and body rest.

Rest wasn't for warriors though. If there was one last thing she could do to succeed in her mission to help the people of Gaule, it was getting those loyal few to safety. She tilted her head back, meeting the eye of each man and woman who'd come with her, remembering those who couldn't stand before her. They were the noblest of Gaule. The best the kingdom had to offer.

And their kingdom no longer wanted them.

"Leave the village as it is. Do not wipe the blood clean from its surface. They will remember us, remember that someone will always fight for those who can't. Tonight, we make for the camp we left in the woods. If it was not overtaken, our horses will still be there. We ride at first light for the border. They will have no more pieces of us." She pushed herself to her feet and took her daughter from Tuck before leaving everything else behind.

Chapter
Twenty-Nine

Coming home. It was as if an entire lifetime had passed since Tyson rode through the rolling hills of Bela or took in the peaceful pastures. It stood in such contrast to the chaos and troubles Gaule faced.

The camp had still been where Amalie left it with a few men guarding the horses. They'd only allowed themselves to rest for one night before riding hard for the border. The village sat at the nexus of Gaule, Bela, and Dracon, and it had only taken them a day to cross into more friendly territory.

Amalie had barely spoken, but her face held the look of contentment as she took in the men and women surrounding her. It didn't take long to realize it was due to the little girl bundled up in a cloak and sitting in front of Amalie atop the horse. Elayne was too young to control her magic. Most magic folk saw no signs of their power at such an age, but El had Basile blood running in her veins. Tyson's father was Viktor Basile, a descendent of the long line of kings of Bela, each more powerful than the last.

The Basile power. Etta once had it, but it died soon after she overcame La Dame, and the world no longer needed the power to protect it from the great sorceress. Yet, both little Viktor and Elayne would have many gifts because of their heritage.

Tyson still didn't know how Amalie thought she could keep Elayne a secret for much longer. But then, Amalie was not a magic-woman. She didn't understand the power or how it manifested.

She'd barely spoken to him on the ride, but Tyson was grateful Tuck never left her side. Even if Amalie never came back to Tyson, he wanted her to have someone she could count on.

On their second day, the village came into view. Before they reached the cobblestone streets leading to the wharves, three riders crossed the expanse. A Belaen hunting party.

They stopped in front of the large group of refugees and surveyed their faces.

Tyson met the eyes of the leader. "Paint a picture, brother. It'll last longer."

A smile crept across Alex's face. "About time you returned."

"Aw, I didn't know you missed me so much."

Alex grinned. "Actually, I was talking to Edmund." He turned to Edmund. "Vik cries. All the time. I think I'm going crazy. He just wants you."

Edmund sat up straighter in his saddle, all weariness disappearing. "What have you done to the kid?" He waved a hand. "It doesn't matter. Uncle Edmund is back."

Tyson laughed. "He couldn't have been missing Edmund this entire time. We've been gone for months."

Edmund shot him a look. "You obviously know nothing of our bond."

El chose that moment to wake. She shifted and lifted her head, piercing Alex with a clear gaze.

Alex went silent for a moment. "Amalie?" He nudged his horse closer.

One of Alex's companions approached. Matteo, Tyson's cousin, examined El with the keen eyes of his. "It seems we have much to discuss, cousin. Come. Our hunt can wait. Etta will want to see you immediately."

"Your highness." The third rider was Alex's ever-present guard. "Who are all of these people? We cannot just bring them to the palace."

Alex rubbed his chin as if seeing Amalie's people for the first time. His eyes flicked from Tyson to Amalie. "They come. If my brother trusts them enough to bring them into Bela, that's good enough for me."

He turned and led the way through the village where onlookers came from their shops to watch them ride by. They crossed the bridge and stopped outside the Belaen palace that looked more like a normal home than a castle. Etta had always preferred simple to grand.

She'd grown up in a forest dwelling so to her, this was extravagant.

They dismounted in the yard as Etta appeared in the doorway. She raced down the steps and threw herself at Tyson. He caught her in a hug.

"I'm so glad you're back," she whispered. "We've heard many things coming out of Gaule and none of them good."

Tyson pulled back. "We're okay, but there's a lot to say."

She nodded and turned to Edmund, wrapping her arms around his waist for a hug. By the time she released him, a larger presence burst from the palace. Estevan took the steps two at a time, not slowing until he'd crashed into Edmund and pulled him into a bruising kiss.

Edmund, seemingly forgetting about their audience, kissed him back with just as much force. When they finally broke apart, Estevan checked every inch of Edmund, making sure he was intact. "We've been so worried. You were gone for far longer than we expected."

"I suspect there's a story to hear." Etta crossed to where Amalie stood at the back of the group. "Amalie." She smiled.

"Majesty." Amalie dipped into a formal curtsy. There was no warmth in her voice.

Etta ignored it as she bent down to Elayne. "And who do we have here?"

Amalie stood frozen, but Tyson stepped in. "My daughter." He met Amalie's fearful eyes. "Our daughter."

Etta straightened, shock coating her features. She covered her mouth with her hand and tears pricked her eyes. "Your daughter? She's—"

"It's a long story."

"Come inside. I want to hear all of it."

Amalie finally found her voice. "If it's okay, your Majesty, El and I are weary from our travels. Is there a place we could rest?"

Etta placed a hand on Amalie's arm. "Amalie, we were friends once. You know you can call me Etta."

Tyson knew what Amalie wanted to say. He'd heard it before. *Royals were not meant to be friends.* But she held her tongue. It was true. Before Etta claimed her birthright, she'd been a prisoner in Gaule, and Amalie was kind to her.

But that version of Amalie no longer existed. She'd hardened herself.

Etta removed her hand and nodded before gesturing to one of the servants. "Show Amalie and her daughter where they can wash up and rest."

Once Amalie was gone, Tyson could finally breathe again. Etta wound an arm around his waist and led him to the steps. Most of the others had already gone inside to avail themselves of the queen's hospitality. The servants busied themselves serving ale and preparing food.

"Just a moment." Etta stepped away from Tyson and marched to where Edmund was peering down the hallway. "Edmund, so help me, if you wake Viktor from his nap, I'll lock you in his room and throw away the key." She narrowed her eyes. "And no, I won't leave him in the room during your punishment."

Edmund sighed. "Fine. But if he's grown while I've been away, I'm blaming you for allowing me to miss it."

Etta crossed her arms over her chest. "He's a baby! Of course he's grown." She smacked the back of his head before returning to Tyson. They sat together on the couch and Tyson leaned his head back.

"So," she started. "I have a niece."

Tyson shifted to lean his head on her shoulder. "It doesn't feel real. I don't know how to move past Amalie keeping her a secret. How do I forgive her?"

Etta brushed a hand over his head. "Do you still love her?"

He nodded.

"Then you'll be okay. The forgiving part is easy as long as it hasn't taken the love part. You just have to make sure she knows how you feel."

"If she doesn't, I don't know what else to do." The story poured out of him. His mother placing the task of hunting down the Hood on him. Weeks and weeks spent living under Amalie's roof in search of the outlaw. The revelation of just who it was she sent him to arrest. The hanging.

By the time he'd finished, Etta's people led the others to where they could sleep on floors or in hay lofts. Better accommodations would be made for them.

Only Tuck remained sitting by the fire with Alex listening

to Tyson tell the sequence of events that led their group to abandon Gaule for Bela.

Etta laid her arm over Tyson's shoulders and squeezed. "It'll be a change to receive an influx of people who have no magic, but they're welcome in Bela."

Tyson met her gaze. "Even Maiya?" She couldn't help but think of how Etta and Maiya hadn't acknowledged each other yet. Maiya once worked for La Dame, betraying Etta to do so. But it hadn't been entirely of her own will.

Etta sighed. "Yes, even Maiya." She unfolded her legs from underneath her and stood, holding a hand out to Alex. "We're going to bed now, but Ty?"

"Hmm?"

"I'm glad you're back." She smiled.

Alex wrapped an arm around her. "And we can't wait to get to know our niece."

As they walked away, Tyson couldn't help but think of how he knew so little of El. She was of his blood and held some of his family's magic, but she was a stranger to him.

Tuck leaned back in his chair, the glow of the fire lighting up his face.

Sometimes, Tyson forgot just how much others had lost as well. Tuck's sister along with his friends Will and Cam should be with them now, yet their chance had been stolen.

Tyson closed his eyes, letting the darkness be his shield. "Do you ever wonder why we ended up here, safe, and they didn't?"

Tuck didn't answer at first, and Tyson opened his eyes to find him staring into the flames.

When he finally spoke, his voice was low. "Every day." He shook his head. "When I met you and Amalie, La Dame had just almost ripped the world apart. Magic folk were being persecuted in Gaule. The people had no food to eat. Yet... you two were the hope I saw. When I performed your ceremony, it made me feel like there was something good in this life. It's why I joined Amalie's fight. But even as we brought food and other goods to the people, I saw the light dimming."

He turned toward Tyson. "The two people I saw pledging themselves to one another would have lit the world on fire before ever being separated. That doesn't just disappear."

Tyson shook his head. "Amalie had made it clear—many times—she feels nothing for me."

"Because she tries to feel nothing at all. She thought that made her strong, but look at what happened. She tried to protect El by giving her up, and it only put her in more danger. No one is ever better off alone."

Tyson opened his mouth to speak, but his words were cut off by a cry coming from the spare room Amalie occupied. Elayne.

He jumped to his feet and crossed to the door. When he pushed it open, Elayne was sitting up in bed beside a sleeping Amalie, tears rolling down her face.

Tyson plucked her from the bed and cradled her against his chest as he walked back into the living room. She stopped crying immediately.

Tuck smiled when he returned. "I'm off to find a place to sleep."

Tyson only nodded as he sat and stared into the face of the most beautiful thing he'd ever seen. Her cheeks were red from crying, but her eyes were clear and piercing.

"Hey," Tyson whispered. "I'm your father."

She blinked, staring at him as if she understood.

"I will never let you down. That I promise you. I'm going to love you with everything I have."

Her eyes slid closed as if his words allowed her the peace she needed to sleep.

Chapter

Thirty

Amalie clutched the doorframe as if it was the only thing that could hold her up. Tears welled in her eyes. Tyson's words surrounded her, filling her with regret. Regret for everything she'd done, for the life she'd chosen.

Not the Hood. She'd never regret that. But for choosing not to allow Tyson or Elayne to go through the mission with her. For deciding it was better to be alone than to put them in danger.

They were in danger regardless if they were with her. She just hadn't seen it at the time.

She couldn't look away, couldn't turn back into the room as Tyson bent his head to kiss El's soft curls.

He whispered something she couldn't hear. Everything inside her wanted to be part of their moment, to belong with them. She'd lied to Tyson when she claimed her love for him had left. It was the only thing she still had.

And yet, she didn't deserve him. His love. His forgiveness. She saw that now in the way he looked at Elayne like she was all that mattered in life. Like he still couldn't quite believe she was real.

Amalie had separated them. Kept them from all they had to give each other. She should have known John was lying when he told her Tyson refused to come. She should have had more faith.

With a sigh, Amalie turned away from the scene she intruded upon, re-entering the room and closing the door.

Etta and Alex were simple people, even as king and queen of Bela. As much as Amalie had fought against any connection to nobles or royals, she knew they weren't like any other. She respected the sparseness of the room. They had no need for grand canopied beds or marble floors.

They'd built the palace themselves with the help of their townsfolk. It belonged to the people of Bela. A simple wooden bed sat pushed up against the far window, moonlight streaming across the soft fur blankets.

Amalie ran her hand along the hand-carved table stretching along the opposite wall.

"That was a gift from Dell." Tyson's voice made her jump. She hadn't heard the door open.

Sucking in a shaky breath, she turned to find him standing with a sleeping Elayne in his arms.

At a loss for what else to say, she nodded. "I suspected as much." Dell was the new king of Madra. He'd married Queen Helena only the year before. Amalie had declined her invitation to the wedding.

Dell had amazing hands, crafting beauty where there was once only rough wood. Amalie had always envied those who could create rather than only destroy.

Tyson shuffled past her and laid El on the bed, covering her with furs. She murmured unintelligible words and rolled over.

A smile curved Tyson's lips. In the dark, the silver light illuminated his eyes as he faced Amalie.

"Thank you." She lowered her gaze. "For getting her back to sleep." She sat on the corner of the bed and rubbed her forehead. "I can't believe I didn't wake up when she did."

"It's okay." He offered her a sad shrug and moved to the door.

But she couldn't let him leave. "Ty." The desperation in her voice forced him to turn back toward her. "I..." She shook her head. "How am I supposed to do this?"

"Do what, Ames?" He sat beside her, careful not to wake Elayne.

"This." She gestured to the sleeping girl. "I don't know how to be a mother. It was never supposed to be me."

Tyson stiffened at her words before sighing. "I've thought about this a lot. You thought I wasn't ever coming back and any child of the Hood's would always be in danger. I don't agree with your decision, but I understand it. Just because you didn't feed her every day and hold her as she cried didn't mean you weren't her mother. Have you ever thought by giving her up, by trying to keep her safe, you were being the best mother you could be this entire time?" He moved to stand, but Amalie placed her hand over his.

"Thanks, Ty. I don't just mean for your words." She swallowed a sob. He deserved more than her tears. "You've always taken care of me, saved me."

He shook his head. "You've never needed me to take care of you, Ames. Even as you stood with the hangman's noose around your neck, you didn't need me. If you'd died, you would have been okay. I saw your face. You were ready to give yourself for something you believed in." He dropped his voice. "I didn't save you because you needed me to. I came because I couldn't live in a world where you no longer existed."

"Tyson," she whispered. His words traveled straight to her heart. When she learned Elayne still lived, she'd felt it begin to beat again. But now, the cracks in her heart had actually started to heal.

Tyson peered sideways at her. "I'm sorry. I know you don't want me to say things like that to you."

Honesty had always been one of the things she loved about Tyson. He cared little for how people would react to his words. If he felt the truth in them, he didn't hold back. He'd always been the least self-conscious person she knew... until she'd broken him.

It warmed her to hear the old Tyson coming through.

"Amalie—"

"No. Say nothing else. I've screwed everything up, Ty. And I know you better than anyone. There are some things you need to hear from me." She inhaled. "For so long, I've thought the best way to face the world was alone. It was something my father instilled in me. Then you came along and I lost sight of everything else. I blamed you. For a long time, I told myself you were the reason I didn't see the plight of my people. But that was wrong. I don't have to follow the Leroy road in anything but name."

"I don't understand." He shifted his eyes away as if afraid to see what resided in hers.

"Ty." She reached for both his hands. "I love you."

His eyes snapped to hers. "You love me?"

A smile slid across her face. "I never stopped. I only lost my way. The Hood will always be a part of me, but I realize now it isn't the only part." She pressed her hand to her chest. "You're here too." Tears slipped down her cheeks. "I'm so sorry for everything. I—"

He cut off her words by pressing his lips to hers and sliding his hands around the back of her head. It only took Amalie a moment before she wound her arms around his back. Every bit of longing of the last few years poured into a single moment.

Amalie once thought being unable to return to Gaule, to continue her self-proclaimed mission meant her life no longer had meaning. She was wrong. This was a new kind of mission. As she kissed the boy she'd married in a tiny chapel on the border of three kingdoms, the boy who'd given her hope after the darkest battle of their lives, contentment settled over her. Home. It wasn't a feeling she'd ever known. Until now.

Until the best man she'd ever known saved her one final time. He thought she didn't need him, that she was strong enough to take care of herself. But the truth was, she'd only broken herself, and Tyson gave her the strength to heal. His true magic wasn't controlling the water of the earth.

It was in allowing those waters to wash them clean of the past.

Tyson leaned his forehead against hers, their breath mingling. "It's a good thing we're already married."

She grinned. "Why is that?"

"Because now I don't have to drag Tuck out of bed and tell him to make you my wife."

"Your wife, huh?"

His brow creased and his smile dropped. "You've been my wife this entire time, you know. Even when you denied me, we've remained connected."

Her hands snaked up into his hair. "I know," she breathed.

His next kiss was softer, letting her know they had all the time in the world. Because they did.

A cry came from the bed and Elayne sat up.

Amalie broke away from Tyson with a smile and turned to the red-faced girl. "It's okay, honey." She pulled El into her arms. The child still barely knew her, but she would soon. They were forever too.

Tyson crawled over Elayne to sit on her other side. He brushed the hair from her face. Elayne shifted so she leaned against both of them. Tyson grinned in the boyish way he had. Even after everything, his face held an innocence she was drawn to. As if he didn't carry around the events of the past like everyone else did.

"Sleep," he whispered, shifting his body down to lie beside her. Elayne curled against him.

Both father and daughter fell asleep with little trouble. Amalie watched their chests rise and fall in sync, not wanting sleep to take the moment from her. A moment she'd never thought she'd have.

She bent to kiss each head beside her and then settled in for a too-short night of watching her world turn.

Epilogue

Edmund bounced on his toes as he stood next to Tyson at the edge of the docks. Tyson smirked sideways at him.

Estevan, standing on Edmund's other side, gripped his arm. "You're going to fall in the water if you don't calm down."

"I won't fall." Edmund shielded his eyes from the sun, peering at the ship as it neared.

"Let me translate what Estevan said." Tyson lifted a brow. "If you don't relax, I'm going to push you in the water."

Edmund stepped back from the edge with a grunt. "Since when did you two become so serious?"

Estevan laughed. "I've missed my sister too, Edmund. But she won't disembark any faster if you stand there acting like you're going to piss yourself."

Tyson grinned. The more time he spent with Estevan, the more he liked him. But it was nothing to how he felt about Helena Rhodipus. The queen of Madra was unlike anyone he knew—perhaps besides Etta.

She hadn't been to Bela since recovering her kingdom in the

Madran rebellion. Etta and Alex visited Madra, but Tyson had been in Gaule at the time.

A dark-haired woman peered over the wooden rail of the bow.

"There she is." Edmund jumped up and down like a child getting a new toy.

Helena's gaze found them and her smile lit up the already bright day. Blue skies hung overhead as if welcoming the foreign royals to their shores.

Dell appeared next to Helena and lifted a hand in a wave.

Edmund waved excitedly. Tyson and Estevan only laughed.

"Why isn't Etta here to greet them again?" Edmund asked.

"Last minute meeting with Alex and Matteo." Tyson heard the conversation between Etta and Matteo when he walked into the palace before leaving for the docks. They hadn't yet told Tyson, but his mother had been making moves. The Moreau lands, which had been taken by a rebellious noble, were recovered and returned to their rightful owner. The duchess was the queen's biggest ally. That signaled a shift in Gaule.

It had been months since Tyson returned and they'd had no word from his mother or Simon. Not even an apology for what her people almost did to Amalie. He'd long since reconciled himself to the fact that a relationship with his mother would only prove more difficult.

He shook off his dark thoughts as Helena leapt from the ship without waiting for the ramp to cover the gap. She landed on the deck with a thud and sprinted toward them. Dell and her guards scrambled to catch up.

Helena launched herself at Estevan. He caught her around the waist. "I've missed you, your Majesty."

She swatted his arm. "Don't you dare call me that, Brother."

Dell finally caught up, panting. "She'll hurt you if you do."

Edmund rocked back on his heels. "You can't keep all her attention, Stev."

Helena laughed and threw herself at Edmund with the same vigor as her brother.

"Lenny." He whirled her around in a circle, and she laughed.

Dell pulled Helena off Edmund and for a moment, Tyson thought it was because he didn't like the length of their embrace. But he was wrong. Dell stepped forward and gave Edmund a much rougher hug.

"Damn," he said. "It's good to see you."

Edmund reluctantly released him so Tyson could greet the king and queen he loved like family. He looked over Helena's shoulder, hoping to see one more person come from the ship. But she wasn't there.

Helena followed his gaze. "I'm sorry, Ty. Camille couldn't travel this close to the baby coming."

It made sense, but it didn't lessen his disappointment. He hadn't seen his sister in years. "Come on. We aren't the only people in Bela who wish to see you."

They found Alex inside the palace sitting on the ground with Viktor and Elayne. Both children crawled on top of him as he screamed that he was being attacked.

It took him a moment to realize he had company. He grinned. "Queen Helena. King Dell. Welcome to Bela."

Etta appeared from an adjoining room and rushed to Helena. "Welcome back." The two women spoke with rapid words as the men watched the children play.

Arms wound around Tyson's waist, and he smiled as Amalie rested her chin on his shoulder from behind.

Dell flashed them a grin. "I knew it. When you took me to the Leroy estate to be healed and Amalie acted as if she'd rather kill you then help you, I knew there was something there."

Amalie shrugged. "I could never kill him. I'm just a sweet young damsel."

A laugh burst out of Tyson.

Dell shook his head with a grin. "We've heard the stories about you all the way in Madra." He leaned forward. "You're the Hood."

"Was. I was the Hood. Now I'm Amalie Durand."

Dell eyed her. "The warrior will always find new battles to fight."

Amalie nodded. "I'm always here. Remember that for the next time your people rise up and demand the Madran crown."

He grinned. "So, that's how it is now?"

She only crossed her arms in response.

"Alright. Make fun. Madran society still works more smoothly than that of Gaule."

"I'm no longer from Gaule. Bela is my home now." And it was. She didn't have magic, but they accepted her and her people, anyway. She met Tuck's eyes across the room. If anyone had told the two of them they'd one day stand among kings and queens and be treated like equals, they'd have scoffed at the notion.

John would have hated it.

But Amalie wouldn't live her life for what other's thought of her, for how righteous they considered her actions.

The party lasted into the night. For now, they would celebrate reunions. Over the next few days, Madra and Bela would enter a new phase of alliance. One that protected them from the turmoil in Gaule or the distrust of Dracon.

Amalie let her eyes rove over the crowd. Kings. Queens. Princes. Guards. All mingling with common people as if it was the most natural thing in the world.

But if there was one thing she'd learned about people like

Tuck or Maiya or countless others, it was that there was nothing common about them.

TYSON WOKE to a pounding on his door. He'd been living with Amalie and El in his small home in the village for a while now. No guards. Nothing to impede them living their lives.

But he was still a prince of Bela and urgent matters couldn't wait.

He expected to find a servant at the door urging him to the palace. When he swung it open, Alex stood there with haunted eyes.

He held a candle in one hand and the flames flickered off his tired face.

"What is it?" Tyson grabbed his cloak off a hook near the door. "What has happened?"

Alex opened his mouth, but no sound came out. He swallowed and finally spoke. "Mother. She's here."

Tyson followed him out into the sleepy village, a million questions racing through his mind. Why would the queen of Gaule be in Bela? Had she come alone, or did the entire kingdom know she was there?

He hated that he didn't trust her to simply visit. She had to want something.

Alex bulled through the front door of the palace. Tyson followed him and stopped abruptly when he took in the scene before him. His mother sat on the couch cradling a baby. Simon hovered behind her. Various guards lingered nearby.

"Tyson." She stood.

Tyson said nothing until his eyes fell on Simon. "Si, it's good to see you."

Simon only nodded.

Alex took the sleeping baby from their mother's arms before she could protest. "You two need to talk. Tell him everything you've told me."

Simon followed Alex out and gestured for the guards to do the same.

Tyson turned his back on his mother and stepped close to the fledgling fire, needing the warmth to thaw the ice in his veins.

A hand on his arm made him pivot. He towered over her small frame. The lines in her face were deeper than he remembered, her hair more gray.

The anger that had pooled in him unraveled until all he felt was a deep exhaustion. His shoulders dropped, and he turned away from her to flop onto the couch.

Not waiting for him to acknowledge her any longer, the queen of Gaule spoke. "I have been ill this past year. That is no excuse for anything that has happened, but we've only recently learned it wasn't only the child growing in me making me ill, but a potion found its way into my food." She sat next to him, careful to allow some space.

"Gaule is not an easy kingdom to rule. Your father knew that, which is why he used fear to keep his people in line. Alex learned the difficulties when he tried to be a fair and just king. But for me, a woman not of Durand blood, the troubles have only increased. I only tell you this because I hope you'll understand how deeply the treason goes within my own troops."

She shook her head. "Anders... well, he was loyal once. His hatred of magic turned him into the monster he became. I never imagined... well, let's just say Amalie wasn't at the top of my suspect list when searching for the Hood. I used the Hood's search to keep Anders and his men busy while I planned the next phase of my reign."

She reached for Tyson's hand but thought better of it and

pulled back. "I have helped Duchess Moreau take back her lands on the border, but that is not all. My loyal units of the guard have been making arrests of those nobles who do not distribute food to the villages. It was always my plan to care for my people, but I am a queen. I cannot go on a jaunt in the woods to shoot arrows at traders and then give the stolen food to the people. I must create lasting ways for them to be fed. Policies and recurring methods, not single events."

Tyson lifted his eyes to hers. "You almost killed them, mother. You allowed the search for the Hood to ravage villages, and it almost took the most important people in my life."

She let her gaze fall to her lap. "I know. I cannot ask for forgiveness for my short-sightedness. Amalie was once like a daughter before everything got so far off path." This time, when she reached for his hand, she didn't stop herself.

Tyson had often wondered what he'd say to his mother should he see her again. Now, no words would come.

Her grip on his hand tightened, and he didn't pull away. His mother was once his best friend. She'd hidden his magic when he was a child and the power meant death in Gaule. She'd planned his escape.

She smiled. "Simon tells me you and Amalie got married quite a while ago."

He nodded. "Right after the battle with La Dame."

"I'm sorry you didn't feel you could tell me."

He shook his head. "It wasn't that. We wanted to keep something just for ourselves. At least for a little while. By the time I was ready to announce it, I'd lost her."

His mother let her hand smooth over the curve of his arm and up over his shoulder. She cupped his cheek. "But you're together now. That's what matters. Can I... I know I don't have a right to ask, but I'd very much like to meet my granddaughter."

"I'm not sure."

"That's fair." She let her hand drop. "But you should at least meet your new brother when he wakes."

"Brother?"

She nodded. "Caleb looks like you. We need to keep Simon's Belaen heritage a secret for as long as we can. He's managed to hide his magic all this time. One day, if Caleb inherits powers, he will bring our kingdoms closer together." She went quiet, and neither of them spoke for a long moment.

"Mother." He closed his eyes. "I want to be so angry. A part of me knows you had no hand in anything that happened, but you could have stopped it."

"I know, my boy. I know."

He couldn't hold on to any ill feelings toward her any longer. Some people said he forgave too easily for grave offenses, but he couldn't stop himself. She was his mother, and he needed her.

He turned to her and wrapped his arms around her narrow shoulders.

"I'm so sorry," she whispered.

He nodded against her. His mother was finally gaining control of the seemingly uncontrollable kingdom. A kingdom that would no longer welcome their prince home. But at that moment, it didn't matter which kingdoms they called their own. Not with family.

His mother held his cheeks in her hands and stared into his eyes. "I love you, Son."

He hugged her again.

They spent the next few hours talking. Alex and Simon returned with baby Caleb.

When morning came, everyone descended on the palace as if it was their home as well as Etta and Alex's. Tyson met Amalie, El, and Tuck at the door. Helena appeared with Dell at her side and Edmund and Estevan trailing behind.

Maiya even made an appearance though she spoke to few people.

Tyson's mother pulled him aside. "I haven't been around family in this way since you, Alex, and Camille all lived with me in Gaule." Her eyes shone.

Tyson wrapped an arm around her shoulder and guided her to where Viktor and Elayne hunched over Caleb, staring into his chubby face.

"It doesn't matter where we are, Mother." Tyson's eyes settled on his daughter. "We're still family. Sometimes we make mistakes—quite large ones—and sometimes we forget just what it is we've fought so hard to achieve. Peace. Safety. One day, I hope Gaule gets to experience what Bela has."

"I wish for that too." She turned a fierce gaze on him. "I'm going to work toward showing the people of Gaule what life can be like. Our fight doesn't have to last forever."

He rested his chin on her head as Amalie wedged under his other arm. "As long as there are things worth fighting for, there will be battles worth jumping in to. Someone will always try to take what we have."

His mother smiled at him and crouched down to play with the kids.

Amalie led Tyson away, squeezing him to her side as she peered up at him through dark lashes. "I won't stop fighting the battles either."

He dipped his head to catch her lips. "Whatever we have to do." He kissed her again. "Whoever comes to rip us apart." He smiled against her mouth. "It's you and me."

She shook her head, chestnut hair cascading down her back. "No, it's not." They'd made that mistake after getting married when they'd returned to her estate in Gaule and lived separately from the people they cared for.

"You're right. How could I forget?" He pinched her side. "I'm married to the Hood, and she takes care of everyone."

"Nah, she only protects them from royals like you."

"Like me, eh." He tried to catch her around the waist again, but she jumped back with a laugh.

"Yep. Evil royals." She turned and darted out the front door, her laugh trailing behind her.

Tyson glanced toward the kids. "Well, aren't you going to catch her?"

Viktor and Elayne jumped up and sprinted out the door as fast as their little legs could take them. Amalie hid around the side of the barn where Vérité stuck his head out of his stall. Tyson rubbed the horse's nose as he waited for the telltale shrieks that would tell him the kids caught Amalie.

When he rounded the corner, they tackled her to the ground. He joined them in their play as the rest of their group streamed from the house.

Tyson didn't know what he'd done to deserve such a life. He met Etta's gaze. Fought La Dame?

Helena said something to Etta and laughed. Saved the Madran queen during the rebellion?

Amalie shrieked again. Saved the Hood?

They'd all been through a lot, but their happiness didn't feel like the ending to some great tale of magic and sacrifice, raging battles and traitorous deeds. No, this was only the beginning of a new story. He didn't know what kind of adventure it would be, but the future mattered just as little as the past. Because right now, right here, he had everything he'd ever dreamed of.

And that was enough adventure for him.

ABOUT M. LYNN

M. Lynn has a brain that won't seem to quiet down, forcing her into many different genres to suit her various sides. Under the name Michelle MacQueen and Michelle Lynn, she writes romance and dystopian as well as upcoming fantasies. Running on Diet Coke and toddler hugs, she sleeps little, works hard, and sometimes refuses to come back from the worlds in the books she reads. Reading, writing, aunting ... repeat.

See more from M. Lynn
www.michellelynnauthor.com

ALSO BY M. LYNN

Legends of the Tri-Gard

Prophecy of Darkness

Legacy of Light

Mastery of Earth

Fantasy and Fairytales

Golden Curse

Golden Chains

Golden Crown

Glass Kingdom

Glass Princess

Noble Thief

Cursed Beauty

The New Beginnings series

Choices

Promises

Dreams

Confessions

Dawn of Rebellion Trilogy

Dawn of Rebellion

Day of Reckoning

Eve of Tomorrow

ACKNOWLEDGMENTS

I don't believe in competing with others when it comes to the book world. Instead, I believe in lifting as we rise, and cheering others on as they see success. I'm very luck to have found a tribe of people who think of life the same way I do. Without them, I couldn't keep doing this.

My family, a never empty well of support. Mom, Dad, Mackenzie, Robin, Doug, Colby, Evelyn, and Owen. You guys are why I keep going.

My wonderful editor Melissa - you've helped make this book what it is... something I can be proud of.

Patrick, my ever-reliable proofreader.

Daqri Bernardo who once again made this cover shine.

There are so many people to thank for lifting me up. Kimberly, Michelle, Linda, Bethany, Genevieve, Rebecca, Lissa... I could go on and on and not thank enough people.

It all comes down to this. My fellow writers have created an amazing community.

And my readers are the reason I do this. So, thank you, from the bottom of my heart.

.

Made in the USA
Columbia, SC
17 January 2020

86899523R00157